S

The Return

THE COMEBACK SERIES BOOK ONE

MARCIE SHUMWAY

The Return, First Edition

Copyright © 2018 by Marcie Shumway

This is a work of fiction. Names, characters, businesses, organizations, places, events, and incidents are either the product of the author's imagination or are used fictitiously. Any resemblance to actual persons, living or dead, events, or locales is entirely coincidental.

Disclaimer: This book contains mature content not suitable for those under the age of 18. It involves strong language and sexual situations.

Cover Design: MGBookCovers

Photographer: Kruse Images & Photography

Model: BT Urruela

Editor: All About the Edits

Interior Formatting and Design: T.E. Black Designs; www.teblackdesigns.com

AVERY

"KEEGAN, YOU'RE SCARING ME," I told my older brother as I balanced my cell phone between my shoulder and my ear while opening the front door.

I knew he was still there by the breathing on the other end of the line so, waiting patiently, I dropped my bags inside and shut the door. It was a beautiful spring afternoon and I had cranked up Miranda Lambert on the way home, singing and dancing in the seat of my SUV; the windows were partially open to let in the unseasonably warm weather. However, no sooner had I pulled into the driveway did my brother call, changing the tune of the day in seconds. Keegan usually called once a month to catch up, and it was on Sunday afternoons while I was relaxing, not on a Thursday afternoon when I was just getting home from work.

"Avery, you need to come home," he finally told me in a soft soothing voice.

The tone of his voice was enough to have me falling into the closest chair with a *thud*. I knew when he used it and it had been years. Taking a deep breath, I slipped off my shoes and pulled my legs up to my chest, resting my cheek on my knees. A tear slipped down my face and I wiped it away before gathering up the courage to ask the dreaded question.

"How long?"

"We don't have all the information yet," he answered. "Just plan on a couple of weeks. While you're here, we'll figure everything out."

"How is he?"

"Tired, but in good spirits. Do you want to talk to him?"

"Not yet," I replied, trying to hold myself together long enough to get off the phone. "I'll be there Saturday morning."

We hung up moments later. I had barely moved from the chair to the couch and put my phone on the small table beside it, when I broke down. I curled up on my side in the fetal position and sobbed. Tears streamed down my face, uncontrolled, and my heart felt like it was literally breaking in my chest. Breathing came in short spurts and my stomach started to cramp.

My father had been the foundation of our family since I was a small child. It had been him, Keegan, and myself against the world for as long as I could remember. My mother had left when I was two and my brother was five. She had found that raising two small children while my father ran his construction company was too much. There was no looking back for her.

I'm not sure how long I laid there, but when the house started to get dark, I knew I needed to get up and find something to eat. Tonight would be the only time I would let myself fall apart. When I got back to Maine, I needed to be strong. They would *need* me to be strong. I wasn't sure exactly what I was walking into, however, I had to believe everything would be okay in the long run.

Pulling myself into a sitting position, I wiped my face with my hands and took some deep breaths. I got up and headed down the hall, hitting the light switch on the way. I needed some comfy clothes, first and foremost. I stripped down to my low-rise bikini underwear when I reached my bedroom and pulled on a pair of comfy black workout pants with a white long-sleeved t-shirt that had *Grind Construction Company* on the back.

Tears stung my eyes once again when I looked at the name of my father's company. The one he had worked so hard to build; that my brother was now running alongside him. It was a good-sized company that employed up to seventy-five people, depending on the time of year. They did both residential and commercial jobs all over the state. My father didn't discriminate; if something needed to be done, he did it and for a fair price. The Cyr name was well-known in the New England region.

Making my way through the small house that I rented, I went back to the kitchen and opened the refrigerator door to see what my options were. It was already almost eight o'clock, so I knew I shouldn't have anything heavy. The mac and cheese I had picked up from a local diner the night before called my name, but knowing I would head to bed shortly, I opted for plain dairy-free yogurt, granola, and some fresh fruit.

As I settled back in on the couch with my meal, I let my mind wander to the first time Keegan had used that soothing voice with me. I had been twelve and my dad had been diagnosed with testicular cancer. Big bad Dale Cyr had had no clue how to break the news to his daughter, and had enlisted his son to do the dirty work instead. It had been a tough year, between the surgery and the treatment, but he had come through it with more appreciation and ambition for life, if that was even possible. The stress and emotions had brought the three of us even closer as a family as well.

Finishing up, I took my bowl to the kitchen sink. Once it was rinsed out, I grabbed a bottle of water and headed to my bedroom, shutting all the lights off along my way. I was emotionally strung out and I knew it wouldn't take long to fall asleep. As I pulled my sheet and comforter down to climb into bed, my cell phone vibrated in my hand. Checking it as I plugged it into the charger, I found the message was from my brother.

Everything will be okay. I love you.

Those simple words meant so much. We would all be fine, as long as we were together. Crawling under the covers, I snuggled in deep and allowed myself one final cry before I put on my brave face. Hopefully, I'd be able to get some sleep.

"What do you mean, he's gone?" I asked.

The words coming from the mouth of the boy in front of me didn't make sense. I had seen him just last night. We had spent our graduation night wrapped in each other's arms. Our group had broken camp just hours ago and had all gone home for naps. We were supposed to meet up for lunch.

"They all left. The band. Signed on the dotted line and packed up for Nashville. I'm sorry."

"I was just with them. They didn't say anything," I stammered, tears filling my eyes. I felt my heart breaking.

"I'm so sorry, Ave. He's a coward."

His brother was right. He was a coward. He had made love to me the night before, held me in his arms, telling me I was his everything, and had kissed me this morning like he hadn't wanted to stop. There was no goodbye. No clue that he was even thinking *about leaving.*

It was hard to breathe. As soon as the door closed to my car, the sobs I had been holding back escaped. The pain in my heart was blinding. I should have known. The band was good, really good. They had connections. He had never been one for the long haul, but how did I tell my heart that? Why hadn't love been enough to make him stay?

My eyes popped open, my body streaked with sweat. It never failed. The demons of my past always seemed to haunt me, never letting me forget the reason I ran from home as soon as I could. No matter how long it had been, I would always have to face my past, which was why I avoided going home. I sighed, closing my eyes again, willing myself back to sleep. Hopefully, this time, my sleep would be dreamless.

The next morning, as I looked in the mirror, I cringed. My long chestnut hair, streaked with blonde highlights, fell in waves down my back and looked perfect. That was where it ended. I wasn't happy with the hunter green three-quarter length sleeve shirt I had picked out to go with my charcoal dress pants, even though both melded appreciatively to my curvy size-eight frame. There was no amount of makeup that would cover my red-rimmed and puffy green eyes, or my blotchy cheeks. Everyone at work was sure to know there was something going on.

Between the dreams that always plagued me when I was about to return home, and the real reason I was going, sleep had been elusive. I had tossed and turned. I had cried more than I had in a long time. I couldn't live in the past. I needed to look forward and think positively, yet the face in the mirror was doing anything but.

Shaking my head, I threw my hands up, sending my Wind and Fire bracelets jingling. I left the bathroom and made my way to the living room to grab my bags I had already packed, as well as my phone and my lightweight jacket. *There's no point in prolonging it,* I thought, as I locked up and headed to my car. It was time to go to the office and face the music, regardless of what I looked like.

I had barely made it past the receptionist, Kelly Monroe,

seated under the Lane & Son Management Co. sign and into my office when my boss, Julie Lane, came in, shutting the door behind her. Her father and grandfather had started the company. I put my bags down behind my desk and pulled out my laptop. I got it turned on and fought looking up because I knew the minute I did, I would break down again. This woman had taken me under her wing from the very beginning and become more than just a superior to me.

"What's going on, Avery?" she asked quietly, when I finally met her brown eyes with my green ones.

"I need to go home for a bit," I told her, sitting down and typing my log-in information. "A couple weeks, at least."

"Okay, you have plenty of time," she replied. I heard her shift and looked up when she put her hand over mine. "Care to tell me what's going on?"

Taking a deep breath, I filled her in on my father's past with his cancer, and the phone call I had received from my brother the night before. When I was done, and the tears had been wiped away, we set out making a plan for while I was gone, and how we would handle things if I had to be out for an extended period of time. The best part about our business was that a lot of information was on the cloud or internet-based, so we could work from almost anywhere if need be.

I spent the rest of the day cleaning up my workload and distributing my client list between the other two members of my department. For the next two weeks at least, I would be solely focused on my family. Packing up my laptop, in case I needed it, I looked around. My desk was spotless and shelves where my files normally sat were empty. Despite knowing that I was coming back, it almost felt like I was leaving the place I had called home for the past five years.

"You call if you need anything," Julie reminded me, as I

walked by reception, where she was giving Kelly instructions on how to field calls in my absence.

"I will," I told her, my eyes filling. "Thank you again for everything."

When I got home, I didn't bother to unload my work bag. It was coming with me, regardless of my intent not to work. I went straight to my bedroom when I entered the house and packed three bags' worth of clothes and toiletries. To say I was anxious to get back to Maine was an understatement. Carrying the last bag down the stairs, I checked the clock in the living room: 6:15 pm. It was a two-hour drive. The weather was nice. To heck with it; I wasn't waiting until morning.

I brought all my bags out to the car and once they were loaded, I did a mental checklist. My mail was being picked up by my friend, Becky, who would also check the house. I had already placed a call to her parents, who just happened to be my landlords, letting them know what was going on. Work was all set. I had clothes, my cell phone, and the charger. Any toiletries I missed, I could grab when I got settled.

Making one final sweep through the house, I made sure all the lights were off and that the front door was locked behind me. I crawled into my car, set my radio to the Amazon Prime Music app playing on my phone, and buckled up. Before backing out of the driveway, I took one final look at the house and, once again, had the feeling I wasn't coming back. Shaking my head of the silliness, I left and headed home to Maine.

COOPER

"You did what?" I roared into the cab of my truck as I headed up the last long stretch of interstate, on my way to my hometown of Dewart, Maine.

"Coop, it's not a big deal," Chris reasoned, his voice coming through the speakers from the handsfree system.

"You lost my fuckin' stuff. How the hell is that not a big deal?!" I questioned, clenching my teeth together.

"We didn't lose it," my friend stated matter-of-factly. "We misplaced it."

"You're pissing me off. How the hell do you misplace a U-Haul?" I hollered, thanking God that my windows were heavily tinted, so people couldn't see me fuming, and all but talking to myself.

"Don't worry about it," I heard, followed by a click, then silence. The fucker had hung up on me.

I had left Nashville three days before, to return to Maine, with only my truck, a couple of bags, and an old guitar. My friends assured me they would finish packing the U-Haul with the rest of my stuff and send it north. I knew I should have put off the closing on the house and just done it myself.

Running one of my hands down my face and scratching my beard, I sighed. I couldn't stay mad at them, never could. These men had been by my side through thick and thin, since we were kids. They had become my brothers, even though I had two biological ones. I chuckled as I recalled how we had all met in detention, when we were freshmen in high school. We had become fast friends and hadn't spent much time apart since. It was hard to believe we had graduated ten years ago, and left, without even one visit.

Looking over my shoulder, I hit my blinker and merged into

the lane that would take me to the off-ramp. It was time to take the backroads the rest of the way home. I still had another hour and a half to my trip, but now I would be able to enjoy some familiar scenery, rather than just trees and highway signs. Stretching my back, I weaved through a couple of traffic lights and finally made it to a straight line of road.

Again, I allowed my thoughts to wander to my friends. They were the whole reason I was headed back. We had started our little country rock band, back when we were juniors. None of us had ever imagined Dark Roads would get as big as it did, as fast as it did. Chris's uncle, Lee Hines, had signed us before the ink on our high school diplomas was even dry, and had moved us all to Nashville immediately.

Chris Hines was our lead singer. Evan Foster played bass, while Matt Waterhouse was our steel guitarist, and I played the drums. We were a rag tag group that played country with a rock edge, and we had taken off. I had a number of ACM and CMA awards, two of our albums had gone Gold, and we had just finished our third headlining tour. However, it had become too much for all of us.

The girl had been a brunette with highlights and a curvy body. Just like hers had been in high school. She had been good with her mouth, I would give her that, but she wasn't her. None of them were. Taking another swallow from the red cup in my hand, I headed toward the stage to meet the guys, with my bodyguard in tow. I felt him put his hand out to steady me a couple of times, and each time, I shrugged him off. I was fine.

The rest of the band was waiting impatiently for me. I could tell by their faces that they weren't impressed with the tardiness. I rolled my eyes at them and pointed my drumsticks toward the stairs to signal them to head up. The lights were dim, and I knew that meant on the stage, everything would be black, and I could already hear the crowd screaming for us.

Sighing, I handed my cup off and started up the stairs behind the guys. My foot must have missed a step because the next thing I knew, I was face-

planting it. I lost my breath for a moment and laid there. A hand appeared, and I reached for it, only to find myself face-to-face with the leader of our band.

"You'd better sober up quick," he hissed. "They're expecting a good show, and we are going to give them one."

I plastered a shit-eating grin on my face and gave him a shove toward the stage. They didn't understand. I couldn't shake her. The alcohol, the music, the women; they were supposed to help, yet they weren't enough. My head wouldn't forget, and my heart wouldn't heal.

The sound of my phone ringing broke my train of thought. I briefly glanced at it and saw that it was my mother. She had been periodically checking on me throughout the trip. Smiling, I hit the button and listened as her soothing voice filled my truck.

"Where are you?" Leave it to her to start with the question, rather than an actual "Hello."

"I'm in Maine," I teased.

"I figured as much, you smart alec," she chided. "Where?"

"I'll be at my house in the next hour or so," I told her with a laugh.

It still sounded so foreign for me to hear the words "my house." The place where we lived in Nashville belonged to the band as a whole. Granted, it was large enough that we all had our own space, but this place was all mine. I would sign the paperwork shortly after I arrived and would be able to move right in. It was an older farmhouse, built in the early 1900's on twenty acres, that needed some work and sat back almost a mile from the main road. The barn had come down years ago, but the space left plenty of room for whatever I decided to do.

"Please let us know when we can come visit you!"

"Yes ma'am," I replied, rolling my eyes, even though I knew she couldn't see me.

My mother and father had raised three of us boys and we were all grown and out of the house; however, she never stopped clucking over us. The night I had called them to tell them I was coming home, she cried, causing my own eyes to well up. It solidified my decision to come back and left me with a deep feeling of guilt for not returning for at least a visit. Now, I had to make up for lost time.

We talked for about half an hour, switching partway through so I could talk to my dad as well. The two of them had always supported us boys in anything we wanted to do, and had been my band's biggest fans from the beginning. Hell, we used to practice in the old barn out back of my parents' house. I could never thank them enough for what they had done for me.

I started getting antsy when I got off the phone with them. I knew I was getting close, and I couldn't wait to get out of my truck and put my feet on the ground again. Not to mention that I couldn't wait to be home. It felt so good to say those words. While I had loved Nashville and all that it had given us, nothing could compete with my home state.

"Finally," I muttered, forty-five minutes later when I saw the mailbox that signaled my turn.

I took the driveway slow. The snow was gone; however, it had left ruts in its wake. I would definitely have to have it grated and taken care of, sooner rather than later; otherwise, I would be replacing the shocks in my Dodge. When I took the last turn and the house came into view, I was shocked to see not only what I guessed to be the realtor's car, but also a U-Haul.

"What the hell?"

I pulled to a stop next to the other vehicles and turned off my truck. Slowly, I grabbed my phone from its resting place on my center console and opened the door to hop down. As soon as my feet hit the muddy ground, I grinned, probably as broadly as I had when we had received our first ever award. The air smelled like spring; wet and full of the promise of new things.

I headed toward the house and heard voices through an

open window in the kitchen. Before my worn brown cowboy boots could hit the farmers porch, the front door opened and Mrs. Hood, my realtor, stepped out, followed by Evan. I stopped and stared at them, both smiling at me. Mrs. Hood came down to give me a big hug. She had been one of our teachers in school and had always loved us. I looked past her at my bandmate and flipped him the finger. He showed me a shit-eating grin, letting me know he knew about my conversation with Chris.

After our greeting, I followed her back into the house to sign the paperwork that would officially make everything mine. The money had been wired to her the previous week, and we agreed we would finish the formalities when I arrived. The front door led directly to a large kitchen/dining room. The living room was off to the left with a bar between. The lower level also featured the master bedroom and a large bathroom. From the pictures I had seen, there were two good-sized bedrooms and another bathroom upstairs. Linoleum was peeling, tiles were cracked or broken, and the paint was faded. It was going to keep me very busy, which was just what I needed.

When we finished, I gave Mrs. Hood another hug and Evan walked her out to her car. With the house to myself for a few seconds, I looked around and took a deep breath. A calm sensation came over me instead of the anxiety that had filled me lately.

"It looks like you'll need some help," Evan said, as he came back in the door behind me.

I turned around and leaned on the counter, crossing my arms over my chest and planting my feet in front of me. We were pretty close in size, yet Evan's calm demeanor made it so I intimidated him a bit when I was pissed, not that I would actually hurt him, but it was fun to mess with him. I was happier to see him than I was mad. It would be nice to have someone around that had been through the fame with me, that was from the same hometown.

"It does, does it?" I asked, doing my best to keep the smile from my face.

He stopped where he was, his lean frame stiffening like he wasn't sure he was welcome any longer. He was dressed just like I was, in ripped jeans, work boots, and a hooded sweatshirt that covered the tattooed sleeve he sported on his right arm. All of us band members had them in some way, shape, or form. Finally, I couldn't hold it in anymore and I grinned at him.

"I'm messin' with you, man," I chuckled. "I couldn't have picked a better person to be here with me."

Evan came the rest of the way into the room and grabbed the hand that I offered to him, pumping it in his own and bringing me in for a bro hug. When we separated, I turned and took it all in. We definitely had our work cut out for us, but the first thing we needed was food. I heard a *hum* and realized the refrigerator was running. I opened the door and found that it was fully stocked. By the looks of the meals that were there, it had been my mother. God, was it good to be home.

AVERY

SUNLIGHT WARMED MY FACE AND the smell of coffee stirred my senses. Rolling over, I stretched and got my bearings before opening my eyes. I was in the spare bedroom at my brother's house and by the looks of the light in the room, I had slept well past my usual time. I grabbed my phone from the bedside table and found that it was eight o'clock. I never slept that late. My internal alarm clock usually had me up by six at the latest.

Throwing back the covers, I swung my feet over the side of the bed and headed for the door. After a quick stop in the bathroom in the hallway on my way by, I headed down the stairs and into the kitchen. I pulled my hair up into a messy bun just as I stepped over the threshold and found my brother leaning against the counter, sipping on a cup of coffee.

"Morning, Pipsqueak," he greeted, handing me a cup.

"Really? Pipsqueak?" I asked, putting my cup in the Keurig and starting my hot chocolate. "I'm twenty-eight, ya know."

"You sure?" he questioned, gesturing toward my morning drink of choice.

I stuck my tongue out at him and moved around the kitchen, gathering what I needed to make myself an omelet. My sister-in-law, Abby, hadn't been feeling well the night before when I arrived, so I assumed she wouldn't be up making anything. I motioned to the ingredients as my brother made himself comfortable at the table. With his nod, I set about making us both something to eat. The quiet and the mundane task of cooking set me at ease.

"Sit," Keegan instructed, as I set our plates down on the table.

Knowing I couldn't get out of what was coming. I grabbed my cup from the counter and sat down across from him with a *thud*. I had bunked with them because I hadn't been ready to see my father. My brother and his wife had welcomed me with open arms when I had shown up on their doorstep, and the three of us had spent hours the night before, reminiscing.

Abby had entered our lives when we were in high school. Her family had moved here from Florida and Keegan had fallen in love with her at first sight. The feelings were mutual and the two have been a thing ever since. They wasted no time getting married and had done so right after graduation. She was a teacher now, along with my childhood best friend, Jennifer.

"As soon as we're done eating, we are going to go over there and see him," he informed me, taking a bite out of his omelet.

"I know."

"He's not sick yet, just tired. That's what triggered him to make the appointment in the first place," he continued. "According to Dad, they did some bloodwork and scans. He goes back Monday to find out the results."

"What do you mean, 'according to Dad'?" I asked, a fork full of my breakfast hovering near my mouth. "You didn't go with him?"

"He wouldn't let me, and informed me that I would not be going with him on Monday either."

"Stubborn old coot," I sighed with a laugh.

"That he is," he agreed. "We know he will tell us everything in his own good time. I figured, with you here, he might be more apt to do so, sooner rather than later."

"Okay."

"Okay?"

"Yes, okay," I replied. "I have the next two weeks off. Julie said we could talk after that, if I need to stay longer, and I can work easily from here."

"Don't go jumping the gun," Keegan chided.

"How can I not, Keeg?"

"We don't even know if there is anything wrong."

"He's been sick before, and they told us it might come back," I reminded him, jumping up to put my plate in the sink. "What if we have to go through that all over again?"

"We'll be fine. Just like we were before," he stated, placing his hands on my shoulders and squeezing gently. "Go get ready, and we'll head out to find him."

Breaking away from my brother, I went back upstairs. I grabbed a pair of jeans and a light sweater before going to the bathroom to taking a quick shower. Twenty minutes later, I was downstairs, pulling on well-worn work boots. I knew my dad wasn't home, even though it was Saturday. He was either on a job site or at his office.

"Ready?" my brother asked, jingling his truck keys and opening the front door.

"Yep," I responded, flipping my damp hair over my shoulder. "Let's get this show on the road."

We left the driveway and made our way into town. I took in all the changes as well as all the things that, despite the years, still remained the same. There was a general store, a hardware store, local diner, a mechanic, and a bar. Though some of the names had changed, the buildings held the same historic charm.

"Willie's Tavern?" I asked, looking over at Keegan.

"Yep, Willie Hall took it over a couple of years ago," he informed me. "We'll have to go before you head back to Mass."

"Willie Hall, huh? Can't say I saw that coming," I replied with a smile.

Willie Hall was one of three brothers born to Jeff and Marcia Hall. Our families had been close growing up. The youngest brother worked for Grind Construction and Keegan had high hopes he would be a foreman for one of the crews soon. Willie, the middle child, had been the quietest of them, but had obviously done well for himself by the looks of the building. It had been newly-renovated and looked inviting. The oldest brother, the one I had graduated with, was now part of one of the most well-known country rock bands in the world. Cooper and his band had made a name for themselves, even if they had had to break some hearts along the way.

"Who bought the old Allen place?" I asked, as the lifted black Dodge in front of us pulled into the long driveway of the home next to my father's shop.

"Dunno," my brother shrugged.

The way he said it had me wondering if he really did know, but didn't want to share the information. As soon as he pulled into the yard at Grind, any other thoughts I had went out the window. It looked exactly like it had years ago, when I had last been there. Any time I had visited prior, I made sure they were quick trips that didn't involve coming here. I had spent much of my childhood riding shotgun with my brother or my father in the work trucks, or on equipment, and I hadn't wanted that to pull me back. I had needed to make a name for myself that didn't have to do with my father or the company.

Keegan pulled his truck into a parking spot and killed the engine. We sat in silence, each lost in our own little worlds for several minutes. When he finally sighed and opened his door, I followed suit. The smell of the woods surrounding the property and grease from the open overhead door on the side of the building quickly filled my nostrils. I took a deep breath and couldn't fight the small smile that graced my lips.

The offices took up the front part of the structure, along with a bathroom. When we entered through the front door, I noticed that everything here was the same as well. The receptionist was off because it was the weekend, but I could hear voices coming from one of the two offices behind the counter. One, I knew was my father's, and other sounded strangely familiar, and female.

As we made our way toward the shop, I was startled when I saw an attractive, lean, muscled man resting against the door jamb of one of the offices, talking to someone inside. My stomach jumped at the work boots, tight jeans, white t-shirt, and plaid long-sleeved shirt rolled up on his forearms, where a tattoo peeked out on one side. Clearly, I needed to get out and date more. When my eyes finished their traveling and met his, my face flamed red. The blue eyes, cocky smile, and neatly-trimmed beard under the company ball cap belonged to none other than little Rick Hall. Only now, he wasn't so little.

"Well, hello there, beautiful," he greeted, straightening and opening his arms for a hug. "Long time, no see."

"Hey," I replied, hiding my face in his chest as he gave me a quick squeeze.

"Get your hands off my girl, Hall," I heard my dad say.

I spun out of Rick's arms and all but jumped into my father's. My father wasn't a huge man by any means, yet his presence commanded respect and attention. His blond hair had long ago turned salt-and-pepper and his year-round tan accented his green eyes and smile. I pulled back enough to kiss him on the cheek and take him in without being obvious. He looked good, healthy.

"Hi, Daddy."

"Hi, my girl," he replied, setting me back from him to take his own inventory of how I looked. "What do we owe this surprise to?"

"I decided it was time for a little vacation," I told him, looking around him to see Marcia sitting at her desk, smiling. "Sorry if we're interrupting."

"Poo," Marcia commented, waving her hand. "You are fine."

I moved around my father and into her open arms. This woman had been like the mother I had never had. She had easily taken Keegan and myself under her wing, along with her own boys. Her husband, Jeff, had been just as sweet. Without the two of them, my father would not have been able to have done what he did with his business *and* raise us. I wonder how much my father had shared with them in regard to his health.

"She might not be interrupting, but damn, is she a distraction," Rick commented from behind me.

I laughed when I turned around just in time to see my brother smacking him in the chest, and pushing him toward the shop. Both of our parents shook their heads at his antics, but smiled. He had always been the vocal one of the three brothers.

"Why don't you all go into your office, Dale," Marcia

recommended. "I'll finish up what I can, and we can tackle everything else on Monday."

My father was so happy to see me that he didn't argue. I followed him into his office, and was comforted by the fact that it was just as disorganized as ever. Papers were strewn across the top of his desk, and blueprints covered a table that was intended for meetings. Suddenly, it hit me why I was the OCD-driven, organized woman that I was; you couldn't find anything in here.

"So, care to tell me the real reason behind your being here," he asked, as my brother came in and shut the door behind him.

"I just wanted to visit..." I started, pulling a chair out to sit down.

"Bullshit," my father called, looking accusingly at my brother as he sat in his desk chair and crossed his arms over his chest. "Your brother told you that I had been to the doctor."

"Of course I did," Keegan snapped. "You weren't about to do it yourself."

"I would have told her when I had something to tell," my father boomed back, jumping to his feet and slamming his hands down on his desk.

"Enough!" I hollered, to be heard above their growling. "I hate that the two of you feel the need to protect me, even now. I'm an adult, and we are a family. I deserve to know what's going on."

My words surprised my father enough that he plopped back down into his chair. My brother, on the other hand, was stifling a chuckle behind a cough. I glared at them both. How was it that I still had to be the mediator of the family? I ran my hands through my hair in frustration.

"You're right," came the whispered reply from my father.

The quietness of his voice had both Keegan and I looking at him sharply. Worry crept into my heart and soured my stomach. The worst immediately filled my mind – that he was sicker than we thought. Tears pricked my eyes, and I had to roll them to the ceiling to keep them from streaming down my face.

"Now, don't go doing that," he mumbled, getting up and coming over to squat down in front of me, taking my small hands in his beefy ones. "I was just feeling off, so I went to the doctor. They did some tests, and I will know more on Monday when I go back."

"I'm scared, Daddy," I admitted. I couldn't hide that from him. I could be strong for both of them, but I wouldn't lie about my feelings.

"Me too," he confided, causing my brother to come over and put his hands on both of our shoulders.

We sat in silence for a moment. My father wiped the few tears that escaped down my cheeks and stood, bringing me with him. He pulled the two of us into a family hug, like he had done so many times when we were children. I gripped the two of them for all I was worth, and basked in their warmth.

"Okay, enough of that," my father grumbled, stepping back. "Let's go get some food!"

COOPER

"SHIT!" I HEARD EVAN SWEAR for the hundredth time that day, causing me to chuckle.

"Need some help in there?" I asked him from where I was fixing the frame around the front door.

"No, but who's freaking bright idea was it for us to pull up the peeling linoleum again?"

"Oh, stop your bitching."

I returned my focus to where I was putting wood back up. We had been slowly plugging away at little projects the past four days, and were finally getting to some of the larger things, like the flooring my friend was currently trying to pull up. I wanted to do as much as possible ourselves before I called in any

contractors. Not that money was an issue, but I wanted the satis-
faction of knowing I had done the work.

The sound of scraping gravel had me looking up the driveway. I couldn't see what was making the noise; however, I had a
pretty good idea it was my youngest brother with the grader I
had requested from Grind Construction. I was lucky the
company was basically right next door and I had two family
members that worked there. It was after four, I was sure, so he
was probably done for the day and had decided to do it on his
own time. Either way, I would still catch up with Dale later, to
get him some money.

Finishing up, I put my tools back into the chest in the living
room and grabbed my sweatshirt. It was warm for April in
Maine, but it was already starting to cool off from the heat of
the day. Evan was sprawled out on the kitchen floor in a
dramatic fashion when I moved past him to get a few cans of
soda out of the refrigerator. Evidently, the flooring had gotten
the best of him.

"Come on, you goof. Let's go out and see Rick," I said,
dropping one on his stomach as I stepped over him.

He groaned and got up to follow me out. My brother was
just rounding the corner with the piece of equipment when we
reached him. I smiled widely. It would be nice to drive in and
not feel like you were riding shotgun with Ace Ventura through
the jungle. He stopped and turned it off, before opening the
door and joining us on the ground.

"Hey, man," he greeted, engulfing me in a bear hug. "It's
good to see you!"

"You too, little brother," I replied, gripping him tightly
before releasing him and handing him a soda.

He looked at the can, then looked at me with a question on
his face. Obviously, he was expecting something a little different
on the front of the can than the Mt. Dew logo he was seeing. I

rolled my eyes and he shrugged, before opening it and taking a long swig.

"How have you been?" he asked, wiping his mouth with the back of his hand.

"Good, the house is keeping us busy."

"If you ask me, we should just call someone to do the work for us," Evan muttered beside me. "These hands are my life."

"You can come by when you're done working and check it out if you want," I told him, elbowing my friend in the gut.

"Sounds like a plan. I got to tell you who I saw Saturday anyway," Rick said with a wink. "I'll just finish up and take this mother back to the shop."

"Pizza from Claire's?" I asked, turning as he jumped back up on the machine.

"Yeah," he agreed. "You call it in and I'll pick it up."

I sent him a thumbs-up as he started the grader and went back to work. Heading toward the house, I pulled my cell phone from my pocket and made the quick call to order us two large pizzas from the local general store. I gave them Rick's name and quickly hung up before they figured out otherwise. Evan and I hadn't strayed far from the house because we didn't want to cause a stir; however, my parents had assured me when they visited that people were already buzzing.

"Who do you think your brother saw?" Evan questioned, as we cleaned up the messes we made while we were working.

"It could be just about anyone," I replied, filling an empty trash can with pieces of linoleum. "I haven't been here in ten years, so anything would be news to me."

A couple of hours later, we all sat around the old worn table, stuffed to the gills. On top of finishing a pizza and a half, we had cleaned out a dozen cookies that my mom had sent over with my brother. I opened a bottle of water and leaned back on two legs of my chair while I took a sip. It felt good to be home and even better to be spending some time with my family. The three of us had always been close growing up, and leaving them had been hard on all of us.

"So, who did you see?" Evan asked Rick.

I shook my head and smiled. He was like a dog with a bone, that one. Out of all the members of the band, he had to be the nosiest one. Evan always knew the latest gossip and had his hand in everyone's business. He was also fiercely loyal and made sure that any crap that came out about us, that wasn't true, was quickly remedied.

"Oh, that," my brother drawled. "This information is for Coop."

"Really?" I asked, raising an eyebrow.

"Yeah, I saw Avery at the shop this weekend."

The front feet of my chair came down with a snap loud enough I thought the whole thing was going to cave underneath me. My heart sped up and my eyes grew wide. Other than the time missed with my family, she had been my biggest regret about leaving Maine. My friend had that shit-eating grin again and my brother's face had lit up. They'd gotten the reaction they were hoping for.

"What is she doing home?"

The question had Rick's face falling. Evan noticed as well and looked at me with concern. I shook my head, unsure of what was going on. I was certain Avery was home visiting her family, but I didn't know why that would cause my brother to look like he had just lost his puppy.

"Rick, why is she home?" I asked again.

"The big guy's cancer came back," he finally said on a sigh.

My heart stopped. I think I felt it lodge in my throat and stop beating. Dale had been a mentor, a friend, and a second father to me. I vaguely remembered the first battle, but we had been young and, at that point, I hadn't been that close to Avery;

that had come when we were in high school. I felt a prick at the back of my eyes and had to close them to keep them from filling. Pinching the bridge of my nose between my thumb and pointer finger, I took a couple of deep breaths.

"He hadn't been feeling right and went to the doctor last week. Monday was his follow up and they found that it had come back," he told us. "They think that they caught it soon enough that with surgery and aggressive treatment, he will be right as rain."

"Fuck!" I cursed, banging a fist on the table and getting up to pace.

"He's scheduled to go in next Monday. He wanted the week to get things in order before he ended up sick."

"I'll try to get over to see him this week," I told him. "Where is she staying?"

"You think going to see her is a wise idea?" Evan asked with a snort.

"Yeah, have you even talked to her since you left?" Rick questioned.

I put my hands on the bar facing the living room, so they couldn't see my face, and shook my head. I needed to see her. I needed her to know I was here for them, for her. I knew in my gut, though, that she wouldn't want to see me. I wasn't that stupid. I had treated her like shit and didn't deserve a minute of her time. I had been young and dumb. There was nothing I could do to change that now, but I could sure as hell try to make it up to her in any way possible.

"Give her some time, man," Rick advised. "She's got a lot going on right now."

"I agree with him," my friend remarked. "How does she look?"

"As gorgeous as ever," my little brother replied with a smirk. "More so, if that is even possible."

"Nice!"

I snapped around and took two steps in Evan's direction before I could stop myself. The sight of him scrambling out of his chair and backpedaling away from me stilled my movement. We stood looking at each other for a moment, before I shifted and headed out the front door, letting it slam shut behind me.

Leaning against the railing of the porch, I took a couple deep breaths of the cool night air and closed my eyes. Obviously, my emotions were high about Dale, but that explosion had been all about Avery. When we were younger, I had constantly been on edge, feeling the need to protect her from my own reputation.

When Lee signed us, I had turned and run with my tail between my legs. Disappearing without even saying goodbye because I thought that was what was best for her. It was a clean break and she could find someone that would be better for her than I was. What I hadn't counted on were the millions of little pieces it would leave my heart in to walk away.

Ten minutes later, I felt in control again and headed back inside. Rick and Evan looked up from where they were sitting at the table, talking. I went back to my chair and grabbed my water. Taking a few long pulls from the bottle, desperately wishing it was something stronger, I set it back down and turned to my friend with my hand out.

"I'm sorry," I told him.

"Don't worry about it," Evan said, shaking my outstretched hand. "I shouldn't have said anything."

"She's not mine anymore. There was no need for me to go after you for agreeing with my brother."

"So, you wouldn't mind if I asked her out then?"

"If you don't mind if I pull a Lorena Bobbitt?" I countered.

The two of them erupted in laughter with that comment. I

shook my head at them, yet the smile I tried to hold back came through. They both knew just how to push my buttons.

"We were thinking we would go down to Willie's on Saturday night," Rick told me as we were taking care of things from supper.

"Isn't he having karaoke that night?"

"Yep, but he alternates it with regular music every hour or so," he informed me. "It keeps people entertained and allows them to cut loose a little."

"Maybe we should wait until things die down about us being here. I don't want to cause problems for Will."

"I'm pretty sure Keegan and Jennifer are going to drag Avery out. Kind of a last hurrah before the battle with their dad starts."

"What time are we going?"

AVERY

"How did I let you convince me this was a good idea?" I asked my best friend, Jen, as I fidgeted with my dark wash jeans and my black knee-high boots.

"Because you and Keegan both need a night out before you have to help your dad," she reminded me, slapping my hand away from where I was trying to pull my low-cut V-neck shirt up under my jacket.

I glared at her in response as we followed Keegan and Abby through the parking lot of Willie's Tavern. Jen had been my best friend growing up; she had been the wild child to my angelic nature. Now, as an adult, she was happily married to an accountant, Michael Smith; and was a teacher, go figure. My heart wasn't exactly into going out, but I knew she meant well.

Brushing her long brunette hair back, she looped her arm through mine and gave me a loving smile. I kissed her cheek and squeezed her hand.

Keegan held open the door for us and I was taken back by the amount of people inside. Michael and one of his friends from the office were meeting us there, so Jen tugged me to the bar to grab our first round of drinks. We slipped into a tiny open spot and my friend's hand went up to signal the bartender. When he turned toward me fully, my mouth dropped open. Apparently, Rick wasn't the only Hall who had grown into his good looks.

William, or Willie to his friends, was all muscle underneath his tight hunter green t-shirt, and tattoos covered both biceps and forearms. His jeans gripped his thighs like a glove and when my eyes traveled up, his mouth held a knowing smile under a five o'clock shadow. I blushed and smiled at him in return, which caused his brown eyes to sparkle under the brim of his ballcap. Sometimes I wondered why I hadn't fallen for him instead of the one who had obliterated my heart.

"Hey, gorgeous," he greeted. "We've missed you around these parts."

"I've missed you all too," I assured him, putting my hand over his on the bar.

He picked it up and planted a soft kiss on the back of it, flashing me another killer smile. Any other woman would have been pooled on the floor; unfortunately, other than an appreciation for his good looks, I felt nothing. Not even a glimmer of a spark. Now I remembered why I didn't date; his damn brother had ruined other men for me.

"Okay, enough, you two," Jen cut in. "Some of us would like to drink tonight."

With a booming laugh, Willie gave me back my hand and

took our drink order. My friend got a mixed drink that sounded like it was all liquor while I stuck to a club soda with lemon. I'd planned to have an adult beverage later, but for now, I figured I'd stick to the soda. Once he served us, Willie gave us another grin and moved to a gaggle of women waiting further down the bar.

I turned and followed Jen back toward the front door where there were tables set up. Keegan and Abby had found the other two and the four of them had pulled tables closer, so we could all sit together. I looked at Michael's coworker and quickly grabbed my friend's arm with my free hand. I knew what she was up to. He was good-looking in a preppy way, with sandy brown hair styled 'just so', and blue eyes. Though he looked good in jeans and white button-up shirt, he just wasn't my type.

"Hey, baby," Jen cooed to her husband, kissing him and shaking off my hand before shifting her attention. "Trent, how are you?"

"I'm good, Jen," he replied, standing up and giving her a friendly hug.

"This is my friend Avery, that I've been telling you about," she introduced, swinging her arm in my direction.

I raised my eyebrow at her as I leaned in to shake his hand. He turned his smile up a couple of notches and I instantly felt bad about the situation. My friend had clearly given him the wrong idea. I moved around the table to sit beside my brother and Jen sat on my other side.

"What are you doing?" I hissed at her, as Keegan asked the guys if they wanted anything before heading to the bar.

"You need to find a nice guy," she whispered back.

"I don't need any guy right now," I told her in a low voice.

She gave me a look and turned back to Abby to talk about some of their mutual students. Sighing, I joined in easily to the conversation Mike and Trent were having about one of their clients. I hated having "shop" talk when it came to accounting, while I was out at a bar. It was *not* one of those things that helped me to unwind.

When my brother returned, we got to talking about Grind and I relaxed considerably. Trent even asked us about the business. He did seem like a genuinely nice guy and he was easy on the eyes, but that was it. Karaoke got started and our attention was drawn to the people attempting to belt out Carrie Underwood and Jason Aldean. I don't remember the last time I had laughed that hard.

"Time to dance, lady," Jen stated, hauling me to my feet once the singers took a break and the DJ took over.

"Yes, ma'am," I agreed, gladly following her out to the floor.

We somehow found an empty spot and happily bounced around to modern country hits for the next hour. More times than I could count, men came over and either asked us to dance or joined in without an invitation. For the most part, they were good about backing off, especially when we pointed to our table where Michael would wave. It felt great to spend time with my oldest friend and just let loose.

The DJ interrupted our good time to announce that the singers would be back with vengeance in ten minutes. After making a quick trip to the ladies' room, we made our way back to our group and sat down in a fit of giggles. Abby still wasn't feeling one-hundred percent, so she hadn't joined us dancing, but she threw me a large smile when we returned.

We immediately got into an animated conversation about our high school days and the things that students did nowadays in comparison. I was so distracted that I only vaguely heard the strings of a guitar from the vicinity of the stage. Only when I heard the opening of the song did I freeze mid-sentence. I reached out and grabbed Jen's arm. The singer's voice was the toe-curling low of Josh Turner combined with the panty-dropping rasp of Brantley Gilbert. I would know it anywhere.

I closed my eyes as the lines from Kenny Chesney's "You Save Me" filled the room. All the other patrons had grown quiet, and I wondered if they knew who they were listening to. I opened them again and turned toward the sound. There sat none other than Cooper Hall. The man of my dreams; or nightmares, depending on how you looked at it. The photos in magazines and online didn't do him justice.

Cooper sat on a stool, holding the cheap black no-name acoustic guitar he had bought in high school. His position had his dark jeans hugging his thighs and had a slight flare where they sat over newer black cowboy boots. The muscles in his forearms danced while he strummed and the tight black t-shirt he sported clung to his pecs. The tattoo that wrapped around his left arm, starting at his wrist and disappearing under his shirt sleeve, completed the bad boy ensemble and left my panties damp.

I heard Jen let out a small squeak and I realized I was leaving indentations in her arm where my nails were digging in. Letting go, I met her eyes and she reached out to grip my hand. My gaze found the stage again and remained there until he was done, but I never let go of my lifeline.

The crowd swallowed him up the second Cooper stepped off the stage, so I took the opportunity and jumped up to head for the bar; club soda wasn't going to cut it any longer. I could hear everyone back at the table calling to me. Waving my hand at them to give me a minute, I wiggled my way around the throng of people.

Finding a hole in the crowd vying for Willie's attention at the end of the bar, I nodded to him and waited my turn. The look on his face told me he knew why I was there when he headed in my direction. I ignored the solid bump from a body behind me and flashed him a smile. I didn't want him to think there was any bad blood between us for him having his own brother on stage.

"What's your poison?" he asked.

"Surprise me with two shots," I told him, leaning on the bar.

He gave me a short nod and moved away. The bump from behind me happened again, but before I could turn around to snap at the rude behavior, two large hands appeared on either side of me. I didn't need to turn around to know who it was. If the memorial bracelet on the left arm, along with the tattoos, didn't give him away, the smell did. All male, mixed in with a little musk, sweat, and laundry detergent; it was his and his alone.

"You should never tell a Hall to surprise you, darlin'," came the low drawl in my ear that had my breath catching and my lower belly twitching.

I steeled myself and carefully turned so that I didn't touch him. I crossed my arms as soon as I was facing him because I knew I would reach out for him if I didn't. I thought ten years would have healed my heart, but when I took in the hat, now turned backwards, and the smile that danced on his lips, I felt like I was eighteen all over again. Only this wasn't the boy I had known. The person in front of me was all man, and a very sexy one at that.

"You lost your privilege to call me pet names a long time ago, Cooper," I reminded him with an edge to my voice that surprised even myself.

"Ouch, Ave," he chuckled. "No love lost, huh?"

Now I remembered why I was pissed at him. I had fallen apart when he left, closing myself off from everyone for the summer before I had gone to college. My father had threatened to take me to the doctor, but I had bounced back eventually. I had always felt like I was holding on to a moving target with him, forever telling him he was good enough for me and that because we loved each other, it didn't matter. Unfortunately, young love hadn't been enough.

"You are still an ass," I hissed, pushing on his arm to move past him so I could go back to my table, forgetting the shots.

"Wait," he said with an exasperated sigh.

I pushed again, only to find myself in his arms, chest to chest with him. His heart was thudding just as quickly as mine, and his breathing was labored. He was as affected by me, as I was him. I tensed; I wouldn't let myself melt at his feet after all these years.

"Dance with me," he whispered, running his hands down my arms and gripping one of my hands in his to pull me to the dance floor.

I followed him, knowing that if I had really tried to get away from him, he would have let me go. Karaoke was still in full swing, but a couple was belting out Lady Antebellum's "Need You Now" so well that some people had migrated to the dance floor. Cooper found an empty spot and brought me close to him once again. I wrapped one arm around the outside of his bicep, resting my hand on his shoulder while the other was nestled warmly underneath his on his chest.

"I'm sorry about before," he spoke into my ear. "You look so damn good that you still get me all tied up in knots."

I shook my head. He could sweet talk all he wanted, but I refused to be sucked into it, though the feel of his body moving gently against mine had my lady parts wet and ready for action. His warm breath against my ear had my pelvis tilting and his hand on my lower back pressed enough to bring us tighter together.

"I'm not one of your groupies, Coop," I told him, though I wasn't sure if I was reminding him or myself.

"You never were," he admitted, softly placing a kiss on my temple.

"I'm not going to forgive you that easily," I informed him, tensing a bit.

"I didn't expect you to," he replied with a smile in his voice.

I let myself relax into his arms and against his body for the rest of the song. I knew what was coming in the next week and for this little moment in time, I just wanted to lose myself. I laid my cheek against his chest on the side where my hand was wrapped around his shoulder and he slid his arm the rest of the way around my waist. We still fit together like two puzzle pieces, like we were meant to be. When he started humming along with the people singing, tears filled my eyes.

"I heard about your father," he said, as the song wound down. "I'm so sorry."

I shook my head against his chest and tried to control the sobs that threatened to escape. I needed to be strong. I would not lean on him. That ship had long ago sailed and the last time, he had taken all I had to give. I put some distance between our bodies when the music stopped, and the crowd started to cheer.

"I need to go," I stammered, starting to back away, and immediately missed the feel of his strong arms around me.

"If you need anything, let me know," he whispered, cupping my face with both of his hands before I could move out of his reach. "I'm only a phone call away."

I pulled back from him, blindly making my way through the crowd to reach the door. I caught Jen's eye and angled my head. I saw her lean down to talk to her husband as she grabbed our stuff. He nodded and gave me a small wave as Jen headed in my direction. Keegan and Abby followed her, my brother tense and ready to fight in my honor if need be. When they all reached me, I grabbed for my jacket and walked out the door first.

The cool night air was just what I needed to clear my head. I had to keep my distance from Cooper moving forward. With everything that was going on with my father, I couldn't deal with anything else. I wouldn't relive the past; plus, I didn't think my heart could take another round with him. It was barely put back together from the last time.

COOPER

"**F**uuuck!" I roared, tossing the hammer that I had just nailed my finger with for the millionth time.

I watched as it bounced off the porch and into the kitchen window, shattering it. With nothing close enough to safely punch, I dropped down on the top step and put my head in my hands. It had been a day. I was ready to throw in the towel and start over. I needed a drink, and I needed it bad.

"What was that?" Evan asked, putting his head near the now broken window.

I growled at him, sending him back in to the room, chuckling. I had tried working inside, helping Evan pull flooring up, but my raging emotions just about brought us to blows. After I held him against the wall by the front of his shirt, I moved outside, and he had gladly kept his distance. Not that I could blame him. The look in his eyes had scared me. I had never had anyone look at me that way before.

Getting up to move and work off some of the frustration, I made my way down the driveway. This was part of the reason I had come home. Any time I needed to keep my temper in check or forget about something that hurt, I would turn to alcohol. The guys had all but ordered me to dry out or they would throw me in rehab. It had come to a head when I stumbled on stage for our last show of the tour, drunk as a skunk.

I wasn't mad at them for the ultimatum. I had been putting their careers on the line, as well as mine. Being famous gave you access to things that threw legality out the window. Drugs had never been of any interest to me, while alcohol of almost any kind had been my go-to.

I hadn't realized it was a problem until the guys had taken it away from me, stuffing me on a long bus ride from California to Tennessee with no vices available. Chris had been with me, along with two bus drivers, allowing them to stop only for fuel. By the time we reached our house and the other guys, I was clean, anxious, and realizing I needed to find better ways to cope with my issues, while my friend sported a shiner, some other random bruises, and four stitches above his right eye. Somehow, our brotherhood had never faltered.

When I got to the end of the driveway, the sun was starting to set. I took a deep breath and let the cool air that hit my lungs calm me. Since I had seen Avery at the bar two nights before, I had been on edge. She had looked just as beautiful as she had ten years ago when I had walked away from her, if not more so. Her curves beckoned me when I saw her and Jen at the bar, talking to Willie. Watching him kiss her hand had set my temper into high gear immediately; the only thing that kept me from pummeling him was the fact that he was my brother. Even now, the idea of another man touching her sent the little green monster stirring.

I knew pinning her to the bar had been a bad decision the moment she turned around and crossed her arms protectively in front of her. Avery wasn't large chested by any means, but her boobs were just the right size for my hands. They had been perfect as a teenager and had only gotten fuller. The smell of cherries had filled my nostrils when she turned, causing my dick to stand at attention and my mind to cloud.

Pulling her in for the dance hadn't helped either. Her curves molded to my body like they belonged there, just like the first night we had been together. Humming had been the only way I could think of to get my mind off stripping her down and fucking her right then and there. Then I said the one thing that had sent her running.

Shaking my head, I started back to the house. Avery had pulled away when I had mentioned her father, but not before I had seen the look in her eyes. They told me everything I needed to know. Sadness had filled them; however, behind that had been the light of desire, and something else I couldn't define.

My body reacted again, just thinking about her. Adjusting myself, I continued my walk and thought about the other reason my temper was off kilter today. Dale had gone in for surgery. My mother had kept us posted and everything had gone as planned. The mass had been removed and they were confident they had gotten it all. As soon as he was recovered enough, they would start with the aggressive chemo treatments.

I hated knowing what he and his family would go through. I had meant it when I told Avery I was only a phone call away. I would do anything I could to make this easier for them. The lights coming from the house as I got closer stopped me. The welcome feeling that filled me gripped my heart and took me back to the conversation I'd had with Dale just last week.

We talked about everything, from family to my fame and anything in between. He never held any hard feelings against me, despite what had happened with his daughter. I think, to an extent, he understood why I had done it; I loved her and wanted what was best for her. The one thing that had stood out in our conversation was not something you would expect to hear from a man to another man. He told me to listen to what my heart told me, and that life was too damn short to let the money and my head lead the way.

Letting out a long breath, I climbed the porch steps and found that Evan had blocked the broken window with OSB we had on hand for the remodel. I smiled and could see him putting a lasagna in the oven that his mother sent earlier in the day. I was lucky he had come here to stay with me. He made sure the house didn't have a drop of alcohol in it and when he needed some, would go elsewhere to get it.

I was just about done cleaning up my tools and heading back inside, when I heard the sound of a vehicle coming up the drive behind me. Turning, I couldn't make out who it was in the growing darkness. I knew it wasn't my family, but I hadn't been in town long enough to start recognizing who drove what yet. It pulled to a stop behind my truck and the motor died, yet no one got out. I leaned against the post by the top step and waited.

When the SUV door finally opened, I couldn't have been more surprised. Avery stepped out, shutting her door quietly and slowly started to make her way toward me. Her head was down, and her beautiful wavy hair hid her face. I put my hands across my chest to keep from reaching out for her when she got closer. All I wanted to do was gather her up and comfort her after what I'm sure had been a trying day, or to take her into my bedroom and bury myself inside her, letting us both forget about what had happened.

"Hey," I greeted softly when she stopped at the base of the

THE RETURN | 45

stairs and looked up. Her face was blotchy, and her eyes were exhausted and red-rimmed.

"Hi," she whispered, wiping her face. "Keegan kicked me out of the hospital, but I didn't want to go home to an empty house. I can go somewhere else…"

I wasn't sure how she even knew that I had bought this house, but I wasn't going to question the fact that she was here. I didn't respond, just opened my arms, and she came up the stairs to lock hers around me. Closing my arms around her, I held her while the flood gates opened. Her sobs broke my heart and I whispered into her hair to calm her, as my hands rubbed up and down her back.

Time seemed to stand still. When her tears finally subsided, I leaned back far enough to cup her face in my hands and wipe away the tracks. She rested her small hands on my hips, but she didn't completely pull away from my body. Moving like one would with a nervous colt, I maneuvered my arm around her and opened the front door, steering her gently inside.

Evan looked over when we walked in and raised his eyebrows. I shook my head to ward off anything stupid that might come out of his mouth. Instead, he silently put another setting at the table and took Avery from my arms and into his. While he helped her with her coat and sat her down, I took the opportunity to finish taking care of my tools.

When I came back in, I went straight to the kitchen sink and washed up. The smell of tomato sauce and garlic bread filled the room, causing my stomach to grumble, loudly. The quiet talk behind me stopped and I heard Avery giggle, a sound that went right to my gut. I smiled and tossed the paper towel I used to dry off my hands at her when I turned around. Making myself comfortable at the table, Avery went to work dishing me out a healthy serving of lasagna and Evan tossed me a garlic knot from the basket closest to him.

The meal was great; the food, the company, the conversation. It was unspoken that certain topics were out, so we stuck to reminiscing about our high school days. Laughter was a constant and as the meal wound down, I could see her slowly start to relax. The stress of the day was still there, but her shoulders came down, her back loosened, and her smile was quicker to grace her beautiful face.

Evan and I started to get up to gather the empty plates when we are all done, but Avery shooed us both away. Shrugging at each other, the two of us headed into the living room while the sounds of her washing the dishes came from the kitchen. It was comforting. Then, doing something we hadn't done since we had been home, Evan handed me my guitar and grabbed his own acoustic that leaned against the wall behind the couch. We tuned them and soon sounds of '90s country songs filled the room.

Avery finished and came out to join us. She sat herself so that she was leaning against the arm of the couch and sang along quietly with us. This was how it had been when we were kids. Jam sessions in living rooms and basements when we weren't practicing our own songs. It reminded me why I loved music so much before we had become famous; the escape from the reality, the ability it had to quiet my mind of every problem running through it.

We took turns picking songs to play. Neither of us played love ballads or anything that had to do with losing someone. Both doing our best to keep it light and uplifting, Avery seemed to unwind further and leaned her head on the back of the couch. I could have kept playing, but as I was tightening my strings, Evan tapped my arm and pointed at the gorgeous woman sleeping soundly on the other side of me. I looked up at the clock and noticed it was already nine-thirty. Nodding to him, I handed him my guitar and got up.

Grabbing all three of our jackets, I shrugged mine on and handed Evan his, along with the keys to my truck to open it for me. It was decided I would take her with me and he would follow with her SUV. I didn't want her driving herself since she was obviously exhausted. Wrapping Avery's jacket around her as a blanket, I picked her up and settled her against my chest. She barely stirred as we made the walk through the house and out to my truck. I buckled her in and made my way around to my side of the truck, signaling Evan to head out.

The drive was quiet. Deep sighs filled the cab every once in a while, and the smell of cherries had my cock straining against my thigh where it was tucked in my jeans. I shifted, trying to ease the pulsing, but when she let out a moan, I almost came. My hands gripped the steering wheel until my knuckles were white.

"Where are we?" came a sleepy voice.

"Heading home," I replied tightly, as I glanced over and found her sitting up in her seat and stretching.

Her arms going over her head had her boobs lifting and a patch of skin showing on her belly where her shirt was riding up. Before I wrecked my Dodge, I pulled my attention back to the road and took deep breaths through my nose and mouth to calm my body's reaction. When she moaned a second time, I felt the precum wet my leg and I shot her a warning glance.

"Where's my car?" she asked, her voice suddenly taking on an edge.

"Evan is following us," I informed her, hitting my blinker to turn in to her father's driveway. "I didn't want you left without."

"Thank you," she replied, sounding surprised. "I should never have come over, but I appreciate your hospitality."

"You are always welcome," I said through gritted teeth as the twitching continued.

I could tell I was starting to get to her. I was probably

blowing it, yet I couldn't help that my body had not outgrown its reaction to her. I put my truck in park and leaned over to cup her cheek in one of my hands before she could jump out the door she had opened. Her eyes went wide and the warmth that had been there earlier quickly turned hard. The feelings she had about our past held strong.

"I'm still not ready to forgive you," she blurted out, straining against my hand. "I had a lapse in judgment and it won't happen again."

"I know, sweetheart," I sighed. "But I meant what I said the other night. I'm just a phone call away, and you are always welcome at my house."

She huffed and pulled away. Rather than piss her off more, I let her go. I had tucked a piece of paper in her jacket back at the house that had both Evan and my cell phone numbers on it. I knew she wouldn't take it directly from me, so I figured being a little sneaky was allowed. The door didn't slam, so I assumed that my friend was right there; however, the woman made it obvious she was angry when she got herself into the house and shut the front door with more force than was necessary.

"You have such a way with women," Evan chuckled, turning back to me after watching her go.

"Get your ass in the truck," I grumbled as I shifted again. It was going to be a long night.

AVERY

"OKAY, JUST SEND ME THE financials for all the Marcott homes for April and I'll get those reviewed," I told Julie as I logged into my Lane & Son remote desktop. "I can hear you shaking your head at me, ya know."

"You should be spending time with your family," she scolded.

"My dad started treatments this week," I reminded her as I opened my email account. "When he's home, he's locked away in his room, resting. I need something to keep me busy before I go crazy."

"I can think of something else you could be doing," my boss giggled into the phone.

I rolled my eyes, even though she couldn't see me, and

instantly regretted having told her about my past with Cooper, and the recent run-ins. I didn't know what had taken me over to his house three weeks ago when my father had had his surgery. Hell, I knew why I had, even if I wanted to pretend I didn't. Comfort.

Keegan and Abby had all but kicked me out of the hospital once we had seen my dad in recovery. I had been up most of the night before, my nerves on edge, and I had gone with him to the hospital. They came before he had been brought out, after having some appointment of their own. According to my brother, I had looked like death warmed over, so as soon as my dad came out and we talked to the doctor, he ushered me out to my car.

Kissing me on the forehead, he had instructed me to go home and get some rest. I had aimed my car for the house I grew up in; however, it seemed to have a mind of its own. The next thing I knew, I was turning into the driveway that, thanks to my brother, I found out now belonged to Cooper. When I climbed out and saw him, it had taken all that was in me not to run to him, but the minute he opened his arms, I was gone. All cautions went out the window for the seconds that he held me and just let me cry.

"Fine, I'll get them sent over," Julie finally caved. "Check your secure email in an hour."

"Thank you."

"You're welcome," she replied. "How long are they thinking your dad will be undergoing treatment?"

"He has chemo two days a week and radiation two days. They are hoping that one round for six weeks will be enough."

"Don't worry about your job," she informed me with a loving voice. "I'll send you a little here and there to keep you occupied, but nothing major. Otherwise, everything will wait until you come back."

"I can't tell you how much that means to me," I said, my vision blurring with tears.

"We love you here. Please let us know if there is anything we can do for you or your family."

With that, we hung up. I spent the next hour going through the hundreds of emails I had from being out of the office the past month. I easily dumped half of them in the trash bin as I could see where Julie or one of my other coworkers had responded. Organizing the remaining ones into the subfolders of my inbox by client, I printed those I needed to the wireless printer I had brought with me.

Having that done, I moved into my secure email and found the financials I requested, so I printed those as well. Once I had all the piles organized and I was ready to review, I stood and stretched. It felt good to get my mind working again, yet I realized I hadn't heard a peep out of my dad.

Going to the kitchen, I grabbed a bottle of water from the refrigerator and a sleeve of saltine crackers off the counter. He wasn't feeling sick, but his appetite was already faltering. If I could at least get those into him, I would be happy. I moved down the hallway toward the master bedroom, knocking lightly before stepping in when I didn't get a response.

My father was on his side, facing the door. The blinds were drawn so it was slightly darker. He slept soundly, so deeply, I was tempted to get a mirror and hold it under his nose. Placing the water and crackers on his bedside table, I grabbed the empty bottle that was there and tiptoed back out.

Making my way back to the kitchen, I heard the front door open and close, along with the sound of someone wiping their boots. Figuring it was my brother, I put the empty bottle in the recycle bag and grabbed a fresh bottle from the refrigerator for myself. Before I could open it, a hand reached out and snatched it.

"Well, hello to you too," I commented sarcastically.

Getting another bottle, I leaned against the counter opposite Keegan and mirrored his stance of feet crossed in front. As I drank, I took a good look at him. Dark circles lined his green eyes and his dirty blond hair was long for him. I could see where he had been running his hands through it in frustration.

"What's up, Keeg?" I asked, concerned.

"Just work. Jobs are picking up with the warmer weather and, as you know, Memorial Day signals the start of basically a majority of our projects."

I looked at him a little more closely and knew that wasn't the case. Sure, Grind would be busy, however Keegan had been working alongside my father since I had gone away to college. They had wonderful foremen that worked for them and most of the employees had been there for years, making things that much easier. There was something else bothering him.

"Are you worried about Dad?"

"Yes and no," he replied. "He's strong, so I know he will get through it."

"What gives? You look exhausted."

"Abby isn't feeling well, so she has had a hard time sleeping through the night," he finally said slowly.

"What did the doctor tell you?" I questioned, suddenly worried she was seriously ill as well, considering she hadn't felt great since I had been back.

"She's fine," he told me with a slight smile. "Well, as good as someone can be when they are growing a tiny human inside them."

"Wait! What?" I shrieked, quickly slapping my hand over my mouth so I didn't wake my father. "She's pregnant?!"

Keegan nodded with a broader smile this time. I launched myself at him as tears streamed down my face. He caught me easily and hugged me for all he was worth, lifting my feet off the ground. They had been trying to get pregnant for a while and nothing had happened. I hadn't wanted to pry, so I hadn't asked them recently how the whole thing was going. Evidently, it had finally worked out in their favor.

"Abby wanted to keep quiet about it until she hits twelve weeks. She is really nervous."

"How far along is she?"

"She is nine weeks now."

"I'm so happy and excited for you guys," I told him, kissing him on the cheek and grabbing my water again. "You didn't tell Dad yet, I take it?"

"No, he had enough going on," he said, shaking his head.

"He does, but don't you think this would give him all the more reason to fight?" I asked. "His first grandchild is a pretty big deal."

"I hadn't thought of it that way," Keegan admitted, throwing his now empty bottle at me. "I was more worried about upsetting him if something went wrong."

"Dad is stronger than you give him credit for."

"I know he's strong," my brother admitted. "I'm just trying to figure out how to juggle it all."

"You let me help. That's why I'm here," I reminded him. "I can help at the shop, either in the office or with equipment. You just tell me what you need."

"I need you here with Dad. That takes that much more off my shoulders if I know he is being well taken care of, so I can concentrate on the business and my wife."

I went over to where Keegan still stood, leaning against the counter. He opened his arms and hugged me, letting me rest against his chest. We had always been close growing up, and had always been straight with each other. Knowing he was taking care of the thing that Dad loved almost as much as us took stress off me as well. I could handle the daily care of our father.

"You got it."

"Just make sure that you keep me posted on how he's doing," he said, putting his finger under my chin and bringing it up so I was looking him in the eye. "Don't feel like you can't tell me what's going on because you know I am handling the business. I need to know."

"I promise," I conferred.

"Pinkie promise?" he asked, a slight grin on his face as he lifted one hand up and put his pinkie out, just like he had when we were kids.

"Pinkie promise."

COOPER

"I T'S ALWAYS BEEN YOU," I sang along.

It was a gorgeous day in May, and there wasn't a cloud in the sky. The thermometer was pushing sixty degrees and despite my desire to be outside, we were working the day away indoors. Evan and I had every window open and the radio was set on our favorite local country station. I was getting better at not cringing every time one of our songs came on, and was actually singing along to one of our latest, "You," as it boomed through the house.

I was working on pulling the remaining wallpaper from the walls of the master bedroom, while my friend was upstairs doing the same in one of the two up there. My mother had just left after bringing us cupcakes, and giving me the latest on Dale. It seemed that he was holding his own, as was his daughter, despite the aggressive treatments. I wanted to reach out to Avery, but I knew I had no right to. She knew where I was if she needed me.

"Through it all, you remained the light at the end of the tunnel," I continued along with the song.

"Huh, seems you can take the man out of the music, but not the music out of the man," came a familiar voice, startling me from my methodical motions.

Chuckling, I set down my scraper and turned around to find my band member and friend, Chris, leaning against the door-frame with a grin. Concern laced his brown eyes, yet the smile on his lips was genuine. He studied me as he moved across the room to where I stood. His hair was longer on top, almost so he could wear a man bun, the sides shaved close. I could tell he had been stressing because he had telltale streaks from running his fingers through it. The t-shirt he wore was one from high school, with the wolf mascot on it, and his holey jeans were well-worn. Here, he was just Chris, not the lead singer of Dark Roads.

Gripping arms in a stiff handshake when he got to me, he pulled me in for a hug. I had no doubt he had been the most concerned about me, since he had definitely seen me at my worst. I gripped him tightly and pounded him on the back. When we pulled back, I noticed the dark circles under his eyes. I arched an eyebrow at him.

"Is everything okay in Nashville?" I asked, moving to grab the water bottle I had set on my bureau.

"Yeah," he answered, running both hands through his hair again.

"Try again," I retorted, snorting.

"We've been worried about you," he admitted, scuffing the toe of his cowboy boot against the floor.

I figured that was part of it, yet I had feeling there was more. Chris had always taken anything that the band had gone through, and put it on his shoulders. While his uncle was a great manager, he still felt like he was responsible for us, since he was the lead singer. None of us had ever argued about it because we didn't want the added responsibility. Though, I was very surprised to see him back in Maine. Chris was the one who wanted to get out of the state in the worst way.

"It looks like you could use some help," he commented, shoving his hands in his pockets and looking around the room.

"Possibly," I replied, finishing my water and letting him change the subject.

"Matt and I left our stuff in the living room for now. Where do you want us to start working?"

Ah, so they were moving in temporarily. Well, I sure as hell wouldn't say no to free labor. Evan and I had been doing all the little demo projects we could, and with the extra hands, maybe we could actually start putting shit back together. It wasn't like the four of us hadn't lived in a smaller space than this in the last ten years.

"Today, we're pulling wallpaper, so pick a room," I told him, handing him a scraper and turning around to get back at it.

"You're just a boatload of freaking fun, aren't ya?" he laughed, moving back to the door.

"Hell yeah, I am," I replied. "Oh, and Chris?"

"Yeah?"

"I don't need a fucking babysitter," I informed him, still facing the wall I was working on.

"Didn't think you did, Coop," he answered softly, before I heard his boots thumping down the hall to the stairs.

I felt a slight weight in my chest knowing that we were all together again. We had a lot of unresolved issues, and I had just begun to settle into life back home. I didn't want to hash out all the bullshit yet. Things had been looking up, I felt more relaxed than I had in a long time, and I was starting to remember why I loved music in the first place. I wasn't ready to look my problems in the face quite yet.

I got back to work and within an hour, the earlier stress had rolled off my back. I could hear the guys working upstairs, chatting here and there, and the physical labor had cleared my head. Having them here really did calm me, even though it made me uptight at times.

When Tracy Byrd's "Watermelon Crawl" came on the radio, we all started singing along without any direction. This was why we were a band. It wasn't about the money, the fame, or the glamour. It was about four guys who loved music of all kinds and could make it well together. We stomped our feet to the beat, singing at the top of our lungs. These were the times I enjoyed the most, and that fans would kill to see; Dark Roads was just a big name for a small group of guys from a small town in central Maine.

Light in the room slowly started to shift and fade, making me realize I hadn't eaten since lunch, and I had long since finished my water supply. Grabbing my cell phone, I found that it was closing in on six o'clock and my stomach let out a resounding rumble to confirm it. I bent at the knees, stretching my back and followed it by standing straight up and putting my arms above my head. While I rolled my neck, I surveyed my work. Three walls were done, and I had two trash bags full of paper. Not bad, considering I had been at it since seven this morning.

Cleaning up a bit more so I could find my bed without a problem later, I heard people on the front porch and the guys coming down the stairs. I wasn't sure what was going on, but I did know that things wouldn't be quiet around here, with the four of us under one roof. Making my way to the kitchen, I found Matt's sister, Lexie, and her wife, Maggie, placing takeout bags on the counter tops, and the other three guys buzzing around to see what they had brought. I smiled at the familiarity of it all.

"Cooper!" Lexie exclaimed, noticing me first.

I opened my arms as she ran around the guys and launched herself at me. She was a petite thing, with long black hair and stunning olive skin. I had always had a special place in my heart for her. Lexie had followed us around for as long as I could remember, since she was three years younger than we were, and had supported us from day one with our music. I hugged her tightly before setting her on her feet and throwing an arm around her to steer her back to the food.

"What did you bring us?" I asked, sniffing the air.

"Don't worry," she said, rolling her eyes and backhanding my stomach. "I brought you your own container of spare ribs."

"A woman that knows the true way to my heart," I told her, kissing her temple and releasing her to reach around Evan for my food. "You sure you don't want to divorce her and marry me?"

"She's all mine, Hall," Maggie growled good naturedly, a smile playing on her lips.

I chuckled and headed to the refrigerator for a soda. After some jostling around, we were all seated around the table, eating and catching up. Lexie had followed us to Nashville when she had turned eighteen. Not long after, she met Maggie and the two had hit it off, their marriage coming just a year ago. Maggie also happened to be our lawyer.

"So, clearly you are all here for some sort of intervention," I finally got out, once I finished my ribs.

Everyone stopped talking and chewing, all of them looking around at each other with wide eyes. *BAM*. I had caught them. My back instantly tensed, and I clamped my molars together to keep from spewing things I didn't mean. Shifting in my seat, I leaned back, balancing my chair on the back legs, and crossed my arms over my chest.

"That's not why we're here," Lexie started to say slowly, always the voice of reason.

"Bullshit!" I hollered, letting my chair come down with a *thud*. "Evidently you aren't getting the information you want when you check in with Evan, so you all came home to see for yourselves."

"Now wait a second," Evan sputtered, getting to his feet.

"I'm not blaming this on you," I told him, trying to keep my temper in check. Alcohol was sounding *really* good right now.

"We didn't send Evan here to check in on you, or to keep tabs," Chris piped up. "We were all concerned about you, and we do still have stuff to sort out as a band."

I felt my body start to shake with anger. As I had told him when he got here, I didn't need a damn babysitter. I was a grown ass man and was working through my shit. Being back in Maine alone had quieted a lot of my problems; then again, hiding from the general public could solve most of them. I hadn't had a lick of alcohol in three months, a woman in almost that long, and my drums were currently collecting dust in the studio back in our house in Nashville.

"I'm fine. It's not like I was that bad!"

"Fuck you, you weren't that bad!" Matt exploded, causing all of our mouths to drop open. He was the ever quiet one that, despite the tattooed sleeve, beard, and bar across his ear, never said 'boo' to anyone. "You scared the shit out of us."

I pushed my chair back and stood. I took a deep breath and looked around. Worry filled all of their eyes and I noticed that Chris wasn't the only one with dark smudges under his. I didn't get it. Sure, I had liked to drink and had women for company constantly, but it wasn't much different than many others around us in the industry.

"How?" I asked, exasperated.

"From the time you started prepping for a show until you passed out in bed the next morning, you were a freaking camel. It was like you couldn't get the damn stuff into you fast enough. Add to that the women that passed through your dressing room or hotel room doors. You were either going to kill your liver or your dick," Matt sputtered, standing up across the table.

"Do you even remember our last show?!" Chris asked, his voice raising a notch as he got up and flung his chair back.

The tension and emotion in the room could be cut with a knife. All four of us were standing at this point, while Lexie and Maggie sat, watching us, waiting to see if we were going to come to blows. Our chests heaved, and it felt like a damn saloon showdown from an old western. I swallowed the bile rising up my throat and took a breath.

"I thought I did..."

"Do you recall falling on your face on the way up the stairs? That you missed more than one beat in one of our first songs ever released? Or the fact that you threw up backstage while we waited to go out for our encore?"

"I stumbled a little, but I didn't..." I stopped mid-sentence when I saw the looks I was getting.

Had I really done all that and not remembered? How was that possible? Stunned, I fell back into my chair. A collective sigh seemed to fill the room. There was one thing that I wanted to set straight, though, something that the media had blown out of proportion.

"I'm not a playboy," I informed them, after the guys sat back down.

"Sure," Chris muttered, a snicker escaping him.

"Seriously," I promised. "I've only slept with a handful of women. Ones I actually thought I cared about."

"That's not possible. You had them constantly coming and going," Evan argued.

"I didn't say I didn't take pleasure from them," I chuckled. "Blow jobs and hand jobs were frequent. I needed the release after a show, but I wasn't stupid enough to put myself or my swimmers at risk for a lawsuit. They signed waivers and Mikey has copies of them."

Now they were speechless. Mikey Finn was my bodyguard, and he had been my savior more times than I could count. Aside from the guys, he was the person I was the closest too. I hadn't realized that he hadn't shared this snippet of information with any of them. Maggie was the only one that didn't seem as taken aback as the others, though I wasn't surprised about that. He probably had her help with the paperwork.

"Well, damn," Matt laughed.

"Now that all that is out in the open," Chris said, looking directly at me. "When are you coming back to Nashville?"

"I'm not sure I am."

AVERY

"So $1,476.89 NEEDS TO BE reclassified," I murmured to myself, as I sat on my father's couch, surrounded by papers and files, my computer on the coffee table in front of me.

The numbers soon started to swim and swirl. Sighing, I put down the papers I had been holding on my lap and rubbed my burning eyes. I had been attempting to work since eight o'clock and it was now closing in on lunchtime. My body was exhausted. Deciding my productivity wasn't up to par, I packed everything up and logged off.

Dad's chemo seemed to be taking everything out of all of us. The night before had been his worst so far. I couldn't get him to eat anything at all and even then, he had been up every two hours, going back and forth between vomiting and dry heaving.

I could tell his energy was fading more and more each time he got up, and was grateful when six o'clock in the morning came and his body fell into a fitful sleep.

I had no recollection of him being this bad the first time around. Granted, I had been a teenager, and I'm sure I was kept in the dark for the most part by my brother and Marcia. Now, I was the one hiding things, even though I had promised my brother I wouldn't. My father had made me swear I wouldn't tell Keegan about his rough night because my brother was supposed to go meet with a new customer, two hours away. Dad didn't want him worrying or canceling. I was stuck between the proverbial rock and a hard place.

Stretching, I got up and headed to the kitchen. I hadn't heard any movement from my father's room, but it was time to try to get some food in to him. I had prepared some broths earlier in the week to give him something of nutritional value that would be easier on his stomach. I pulled one of the containers from the refrigerator and popped it in to the microwave while I fished around in the cupboard for a travel mug. We had found that using a travel mug not only made it easier for him to hold it, but also kept it warmer longer when he couldn't drink it right away.

As the broth continued to heat, I pulled a bottle of water and a yogurt out of the refrigerator as well. I tucked them both in the front pocket of my hooded Grind sweatshirt, along with a spoon. When the *ding* came, signaling the microwave was done, I filled the mug. With the broth and his pill box, I made my way to his room. I was extremely grateful it was the weekend so that I didn't have to try to get him moving to head to the hospital.

I knocked lightly before entering and was surprised to find my dad watching TV, and slightly elevated. He smiled at me weakly, but made no effort to move. I handed him his pills and the bottle of water. While he swallowed his doses, I placed everything else on the nightstand and sat down near his feet.

"How ya feeling?" I asked hesitantly.

"Better than last night," he told me, reaching to put the water down and taking the broth; that effort alone leaving him winded.

"That's good," I said, forcing cheer in to my voice that I didn't feel.

"You're so full of crap, young lady," he chuckled, making himself comfortable once again. "I'm sorry you had to see your old man like that."

"It's all part of it," I reminded him. "I get it."

"Doesn't make it any easier on either of us," he responded, taking a sip from his mug. "Did your brother make it down to meet with Carlisle?"

"In other words, did I tell him?" I laughed. My father had always turned words around to find out what he really wanted without actually asking. "Yes, they made it down there, and he and Abby are using it as an excuse to spend some time together."

"Good for them." He nodded approvingly. "They deserve it. You should get out soon too."

"I'm fine, Dad," I assured him. "You need someone here with you."

I got the stink eye for that comment, but he backed off and let it go. I made sure he was all set with everything else before returning to the kitchen to make my own lunch. It was a cold rainy spring day, and soup sounded perfect. While I warmed up some chicken noodle, I rested my head against the cupboards and closed my eyes. An afternoon nap was sounding pretty good too.

A few minutes later, my phone vibrated on the coffee table just as I sat down with my soup and a bottle of water. It was a text message from Jen that was a simple ❤, and it brought tears to my eyes. The message was meant to let me know that she was there if I needed her, and that she loved me. I was so lucky that I still had her in my life after all these years. She was one of the things I missed the most in Maine, other than my family.

I returnd her back a message in kind and set the TV on the Hallmark Channel. One of my favorite movies was on. It was about a woman who returned to her hometown after years away, and finds that her high school sweetheart is now widowed with a son. If only real life was as simple as it was on the big screen.

After eating my soup, with my belly full and warm, I grabbed the throw blanket from the back of the couch and snuggled into it. The sweet down-home air on the screen lulled me into a catatonic state. I was just about asleep when I thought I heard something. The second time it happened, I knew I wasn't imagining things.

Thump. Thump.

"Dad!" I hollered, jumping off the couch, nearly tripping over my blanket in my haste to get to him.

The bedroom door stood open, but the bathroom one was closed. Without thinking, I barged in. What I found had my heart in my throat and tears instantly pricking my eyes. My father was on the floor on his side with one arm and one leg tucked under him at odd angles. I couldn't tell if anything was broken, and the look on his face was one of pure defeat. Before I could get to him, his words stopped me.

"Call Cooper," he rasped.

I turned around and ran back to the living room to grab my cell phone. I could barely see through my tears as I searched in my contact list for his number. When I had found it in my jacket after that night with him and Evan, I had almost thrown it away. I wanted nothing to do with him again, yet something had told me to put it in my phone just in case. Now, I couldn't be more glad that I had it. I clicked on his number and stumbled back to my father.

"Cooper Hall," came his greeting, seconds later.

"Coop," I rushed, my voice shaking. "I need your help, *now.*"

"Avery?" he questioned. "What's wrong?"

"My dad…he fell…I can't lift him," I sobbed, crumpling next to him on the bathroom floor and gripping the hand I could reach in mine.

"Baby, it's okay," he crooned into the phone. I could hear him conversing with what sounded like multiple guys while he kept me on the line, and then his truck starting. "We're coming. Do we need to call rescue? Is he breathing and conscious?"

"He's conscious," I answered, looking down at Dad as he shook his head slightly to the rescue comment. "No rescue."

"Keep talking to me, Ave," Cooper requested. "How has he been?"

"Last night was rough for both of us, but he seemed to have been feeling better when I brought lunch in to him," I told him, the fear slowly starting to subside and the tightness in my chest loosening.

"Almost there," he said. "God, when did this drive get so long, dammit!"

I couldn't help but giggle a little at his exasperation, and I saw the corners of my dad's mouth lift a bit. I squeezed his hand as we waited with Cooper on the line to drive the last couple of minutes to our house. He squeezed back and closed his eyes. There was no sign of pain on his pale face, just complete fatigue.

Finally, after what felt like hours, I heard multiple vehicles pull in the driveway. The sound of doors slamming and boot-clad feet echoed in my ear as I still held my cell phone. When four large, tattooed, rugged men filled the bathroom doorway, I brought it down at last. They were all wearing well-worn jeans with hooded sweatshirts, and I then realized I knew what guardian angels looked like. Cooper tucked his own phone in his pocket before coming over and pulling me to my feet.

"Go make sure his bed is ready for him," he said in a low soothing voice as he gathered me in his arms and kissed my temple. "We'll get him up and bring him in."

I wanted to argue as he moved me toward the door, but I knew my father wouldn't want me to see them wrestling to get him off the floor. I trusted all four of these men, and had no doubt they would take care of him just as they would their own family. Rushing to the bedroom, I heard their murmured voices behind me and shuffling as they shifted around. I made sure the comforter and sheets were turned down enough that we wouldn't have to jostle him to cover him back up. Then I waited.

Again, minutes felt like hours. Evan came into the room first, with a reassuring smile. Chris followed at an angle with one of my father's arms slung around his shoulders while the other was over Cooper's. The three were laughing about something and Matt followed, making sure that the other two were all set. They had a good grip on my dad, but they let him shuffle his feet, so he didn't feel completely helpless; for that, I was grateful.

Somehow, they got him into bed and covered without my help. The chatter never stopped. While they had him occupied, I cleaned up the empties from lunch and returned with a new bottle of water and a sleeve of saltines. When I returned, the guys said their goodbyes and filed out.

"How you doin'?" I asked my father, fussing over his blankets as he settled in to sleep.

"I'm fine," he assured me, closing his eyes. "I just lost my footing and my energy."

Shaking my head, I kissed his forehead and headed to the door. Taking one last look at him, I stepped into the hallway and closed the door behind me. I could hear the band in the living room talking quietly. When I entered the room, they stopped, and all eyes turned on me.

"Thank you guys, so much," I gushed, clasping my hands in front of me. "I appreciate the help more than you will ever know."

"Anytime," Evan assured me, as he came over and gave me a hug.

"You have Coop's number. Use it if you need us," Chris ordered, kissing me on the cheek and squeezing my arm.

"Maggie and Lexie are home too," Matt let me know, when it was his turn. "Call my parents' house if you need them."

The guys headed out the door and I was surprised when Cooper closed it, coming back to stand in front of me. I was trying my hardest to keep it together until they had all cleared out. My hands were shaking as I wrung them together and my eyes were burning with unshed tears. I kept them trained to the floor and slowly swallowed as my stomach threatened to send the soup back up. If he reached for me, I was doomed. I wanted to stay mad at him. I didn't want to need his comfort.

"Ave," he whispered, the sound settling on my skin like a gentle caress.

"Don't," I choked, bringing one hand up to cover my mouth and hold in a sob.

"Let it go," Cooper soothed, bringing me against his chest and wrapping me in his arms. "Let it all go."

The words and his warm body against mine was all it took for my resolve to break. Tears came streaming down my face and sobs tore from my body. I brought my hands up and gripped his sweatshirt in an effort to keep myself grounded. I felt like my whole world was crashing down around me. Everything that I had cherished and worked so hard for was falling apart, including my vow to stay away from this man.

"I got you, baby," he murmured against my temple as he ran his hands up and down my back.

"That's what scares me," I sniffled when I could breathe again.

Despite the years I had worked at building a wall around my heart to protect myself from men, it took just one to bring it all down. The same one who had caused me to build them in the first place. He needed to return to Nashville or I needed to go to Massachusetts. Things needed to go back to the way they had been. I had been happy, at least I thought I'd been. Now I didn't know. One thing I *did* know was that I wanted to forget about everything going on. I wanted a couple hours to just forget that my dad was sick and that I wasn't sure where my future was heading.

I pushed on the solid wall that was Cooper, catching him off guard, and sent him stumbling back onto the couch. I followed, straddling him and bringing us core to core. His eyes grew dark and wide, while his member danced against the denim and cotton between us. My panties grew damp just from the friction of his pelvis' involuntary reaction to my body. Cooper's hands came up to rest lightly on my hips, holding me in place, confusion written all over his handsome face.

Putting one hand behind his head on the couch to brace myself, I leaned in and used the other hand to cup his bearded cheek while my mouth crashed down on his. There was no hesitation as his mouth opened and his tongue dueled with mine. He met me lick for lick and my core pulsed against his from the heat of it. This was no sweet, getting-to-know-you-again kiss; it was hot and mind-blowing. His fingers dug into my hips as I rocked against him, trying to ease the need that was building.

I sucked his tongue into my mouth, eliciting a moan from

deep within his muscled body. He pressed his dick against my core in response. I ran my hand down his defined pecs and the six-pack I knew were hiding beneath his Carhartt sweatshirt, to cup him through his jeans. Even though his body was happily obliging to my caresses and my mouth, I could sense Cooper's brain start to kick in and pull back.

"Please, Coop," I pleaded in a whisper when he pulled his mouth away from mine and loosened his grip. "I want to forget everything that's going on right now."

The pleading must have broken his control because the next thing I knew, he was picking me up and carrying me to the loveseat on the other side of the room. He set me down and I knew that from where I was, I couldn't be seen from the hallway and neither could he until someone actually entered the room. Cooper was making sure my father didn't see us if he got up. When I reached up to grab his sweatshirt and pull him back down on top of me, he shook his head.

"Pants off," he demanded, as he pulled his sweatshirt off over his head.

It took me a minute to register his request as I had caught sight of his happy trail where his t-shirt rode up. I itched to touch it, but quickly pulled my leggings and underwear down while Cooper got down on his knees between my legs. He wasn't going to give me exactly what I wanted, which was for him to bury himself inside me and screw me until I forgot who I was, but his mouth on me was the next best thing.

Cooper grabbed some of the throw pillows and helped me brace myself up, moving me so that my ass was on the edge of the cushion. He picked up my legs and placed my feet on his shoulders while he slid his sweatshirt underneath me. I wiggled in anticipation as his warm breath danced across my thighs. Never being one to wait, his fingers quickly found my folds and opened them for his exploration.

"So wet," he murmured, trailing kisses up my left leg and stopping just short of where I needed him.

"Cooper," I moaned, clenching fists beside my hips.

More kisses, this time up my right leg. I lifted my pelvis toward his mouth to get him to move faster. His chuckle vibrated against my lips as he adjusted my legs and brought his mouth down to where his fingers still held me exposed. Tingling in my lower back and belly signaled that my orgasm was ridiculously close for how little he had touched me.

The first stroke of his tongue against me had my hips soaring off the couch. One of his hands came up to hold me down while the other slid under to cup my butt cheek, bringing my body up so he could feast on me. His licking became more insistent, every once in a while sliding up to twirl against my clit. I pumped against his hand and his mouth, deliriously searching for the thing that was just out of reach.

"You taste so fucking good, Ave," he growled into my folds, as he removed his hand that had been holding my hips in place.

I purred in response as I felt him slip a finger inside of me while he gently sucked at my sensitive nub. Moving my hands between my legs, I gripped his hair and held him to me. I could feel the pressure building and didn't want him to let up. Cooper obviously had no intentions of slowing down, as his sucking became stronger and one finger turned into two.

Releasing one hand from the death grip I had on his hair, I reached over to grab the remaining pillow and shove it against my face. I had always been a screamer with Cooper and now wouldn't be any different. I was almost there, when he curled his fingers against that special spot and hummed. I felt myself rise off the couch as I released a muffled moan into the pillow.

Stars and white light blurred my vision as he continued to work me with his mouth and his fingers. When I didn't think I could take any more, he pulled away. He gently moved my legs, placing my feet on the floor, and got up. My whole body was a pile of mush. The thought that someone could walk in the front door at any moment and see me laying spread eagle was only a fleeting one.

With a chuckle, Cooper moved the pillow that was now resting on my face since my lax fingers couldn't hold it. I could feel his eyes on me as he cleaned me up with a warm washcloth and wiped me down with a dry one, but the energy to open mine escaped me. Moments later, I felt my underwear and my leggings being pulled up my legs.

"Sweetheart, you're going to have to help me a bit here," Cooper whispered, as he tugged them to my thighs.

"Mmmmm hmmmmm," I mumbled, lifting my ass just enough for him to slide them all the way up.

I didn't even get a chance to put it back down before I was being scooped into strong arms and braced against a warm chest. I nuzzled into him and inhaled the scent that was only his. One that relaxed me further, if that was even possible. When he tried to set me down again, I held fast; I was not ready to return to reality. A kiss to my forehead had me sighing and releasing.

I opened my eyes slightly to find that he had laid me down on the couch and was covering me with the throw I had been wrapped in earlier. A bottle of water and my phone sat on the coffee table within reach, and Cooper was heading back down the hall. Closing them again, I figured I would rest until he returned.

"I'm heading out, Ave." His warm voice filled my ear.

"Dad?" I questioned, opening my eyes and shifting to get up.

"Relax," he said, putting his hand on me to keep me from moving. "I just checked on him. He's sleeping soundly."

"Thank you."

"No, Ave, thank *you* for trusting me," he replied, leaning

down to brush a kiss across my lips and adjust the blanket. "Get some rest. Call if you need me again."

Before I could register what he had said, he was gone. I could still smell him on me and I could taste the mixture of myself and mint on my lips from his kiss. I fell into a deep sleep, the best I'd had since I had returned home. My dreams were filled with a handsome tattooed drummer and all the delicious things I could do to him. He might have run while I was in my orgasm-induced haze, but Cooper Hall and I were far from done. At least for awhile, I wanted to be one of his groupies.

COOPER

"OKAY, SO WE HAVE A bunch of people bringing crock pot stuff, your mother is making up numerous platters, and Jen is organizing some women to set up meals for Avery to take home with her for the entire family," Lexie rattled off, with a clipboard in her hand, making notes as she talked.

"Perfect," I told her as I worked on putting together my drums on the stage at my brother's bar. "Chris is on the horn, getting word out around town, and we may have called in some favors for some extra donations."

"You guys are the best! I'll check with Willie about where to put the extra tables, and make sure we are all set on silverware, plates, and napkins," she said, walking away to track him down in his office.

Chuckling, I finished my setup. I don't know if my brother knew what he had been getting into when he offered for us to have Dale's benefit here. Then again, maybe I hadn't known what I was getting into when I had put Lexie in charge. She was crazy organized, a stickler for details, and loved Avery and her family as much as we did. Despite her drill sergeant attitude, she was a perfect fit.

While the guys and I had been standing in the Cyrs' living room the prior weekend, waiting for Avery, we had come up with the idea. After helping with Dale, the guys had wanted to do something, and Evan had instantly mentioned doing a bene-fit. The others had readily agreed and here we were. We had put it all together in under a week, after Willie had offered for us to use his space. All proceeds would go the Cyr family and Dark Roads was going to play most of the evening.

Every time I thought about that night, I had mixed emotions. I was sad that Dale was even in that position, grateful that me and the boys had been able to help, and elated I had been able to bring her some comfort. I should have felt bad about taking advantage of her when she was vulnerable, but the memory of her taste, and the feel of her body under my hands gave me an instant hard-on. I had gone home that night with the worst case of blue balls I had ever had. Jerking off in a cold shower hadn't even relieved the ache I had for that woman.

"Cooper!" I heard Lexie yell.

Shifting the bulge in my pants, I made my way toward Willie's office. When I got to the doorway, I leaned on the jamb and laughed at the mock exasperated look on my brother's face. He was leaning back in his computer chair with his arms crossed, causing his muscles and tattoos to dance, while giving the impression he was pissed; however, I could see the slight curve of one corner of his lips. Most women would swoon over the way he was sitting, but Lexie was unaffected, other than looking ticked off.

"What's up?" I asked, trying to hide my smirk.

"Willie is being a pain in the butt," she stated.

"This woman wants to turn my bar into a spa," he shot back.

"I was simply suggesting massage chairs as a means for everyone to relax," she snapped.

"Lexie, let's draw the line there," I told her with my most charming smile. "Food, drink, and music will be plenty. Plus, we are hoping for a fairly large crowd, and we will need the space."

"Fine." She caved with a huff, getting up and brushing past me. "I'm going to go check on some last-minute details. I'll see you here early Saturday for soundcheck, and to get everything ready!"

"Hard to believe she used to be timid and quiet," Willie commented as he straightened in his chair and put his arms on his desk, with his hands clasped. "You ready for this?"

"Ready for what?" I asked, moving to fill Lexie's vacated seat.

"Playing for a crowd, the alcohol, the questions," he counted off on his fingers.

"As much as I could use a drink, I'm not worried about the alcohol or playing for this type of crowd," I told him, rolling my eyes.

"How about people quizzing you? The talk behind your back? The accusations?"

"I know the truth, and so does the band. What other people say doesn't get to me."

"Hmm," he pondered. "Now that makes me wonder. Are you home for good, big brother?"

"That's still up in the air, and I have obligations back in Nashville," I said, getting up and heading back out front.

I wasn't ready to share my plans with anyone just yet. The details still needed to be ironed out. After what had happened over the weekend, I knew what I wanted. It was just a matter of getting all my ducks in a row and making it happen.

"Shit!" Evan exclaimed, a couple days later, as a string on his guitar snapped with a loud *ping!*

"Break time," Chris announced, when Evan stomped off the stage.

We had been doing a soundcheck for the last hour, and nothing seemed to be going right. The mics were echoing, we were blowing fuses left and right, Matt couldn't seem to get his steel guitar in tune, and I had broken my favorite set of drumsticks. Sighing, I stuck the sticks I'd been using in my back pocket and hopped off the stage. I headed over to the bar where my brothers were stocking.

"Dark Roads doesn't seem to like Willie's Tavern, huh?" my youngest brother joked, handing me a bottle of water.

"Seems that way," I said, after I took a long pull from the bottle. "I would be just as happy doing a long acoustic set."

"Chris likes the show," Matt told him as he came up and leaned his back on the bar, facing the stage.

"Some things never change," Willie retorted as he unboxed beer and filled the minifridges on the floor.

I had barely registered the front door opening while we were talking, but when my peripheral vision caught sight of a certain curvy brunette, my cock jumped to attention. A picture of her screaming into a pillow, with her legs spread wide open for me flashed in my mind as she and Jen drew near. Avery was outfitted in a hunter green fleece jacket with the Grind emblem, dark skinny jeans, and her black knee-high boots. My eyes followed her every move and the gentle sway of her hips. When I finally reached her face, I found her cheeks with a slight flush, her eyes sparkling, and a knowing secret smile teasing her lips.

"Like I said, some things never change," my brother muttered, before setting a full box down a little too hard with a *cling!*

I snapped my head around and looked at Willie, my eyebrows raised. I wasn't sure what had suddenly crawled under his skin, but I didn't like what he was insinuating. Avery wasn't just any woman. She was everything to me and always had been, even though others thought I was the king of sleeping around. No one affected me the way she did.

"Well, hello beautiful ladies," Rick greeted when they reached us.

"Hi, Ricky Bobby," Jen returned with a grin and a wink.

The movie reference had everyone laughing, except my brother. Ever since Talladega Nights had come out, people had been calling him Ricky Bobby and it drove him crazy. If it had been anyone other than our childhood friend using it, he would have been over the bar and giving them what-for. She leaned over the bar to give him a kiss on the cheek to ease the blow and he smirked at her.

"Can we talk?" I jumped at the question and the hand on my arm; I hadn't seen her move to my side.

I nodded and took her hand in mine to lead her down the hall behind the bar. We stopped just outside of Willie's office and I leaned against the wall, so I didn't invade her space. I stuck my hands in my pockets since I itched to touch her, giving the impression that I was completely relaxed. If she looked hard enough though, she wouldn't miss the hard length in my pants.

"I wanted to thank you for the other day," she said, her voice low as she moved closer to me, putting her hand on my stomach. It burned me through the cotton and I sucked in a breath.

"Of course; we love your dad," I told her, not moving a muscle in my body.

"No"–she shook her head–"I was talking about what you did for *me*."

The pink in her cheeks deepened and my dick twitched. Her tongue darted out to wet her lips and her breathing became labored. I clenched my jaw to try to keep myself under control. One more touch, or another signal from her, and I was going to snap. When her other hand came up and rested on my pec, I lost it.

Grabbing her hands in mine, I spun us and pinned her to the wall with my body, her hands above her head. Her eyes had widened, darkening with lust. I ran my free hand down her hip and around to cup her perfect ass, pulling her tighter against my shaft straining in my jeans. There was no mistaking it now. I wanted her, and she knew it.

"I was hoping we could do it again," she breathed as I ran my lips lightly across hers and down to her neck.

"Oh," I answered between nibbles, "that could definitely be arranged."

"We will have to set some boundaries," she stammered, as her hips ground against mine. "No strings attached. No commitments. No feelings."

I froze for a second. She just wanted sex. My sweet little Avery just wanted to use my body to forget all of her problems. No emotions involved. Well, we would have to see about that. I was up for a challenge, especially if it was her.

"Be ready tonight," I told her before crashing my mouth onto hers.

She gasped as I let go of her hands and grabbed her ass,

lifting her to wrap her legs around me. I dove my tongue into her mouth when she opened it, and rubbed hard against her as she locked her ankles at my lower back. I thought I was going to blow my load at the friction her continued pumps were causing. Avery met me stroke for stroke as our mouths mimicked what we wanted to truly be doing. I braced her back against the wall and slid one of my hands up under her jacket, the cami she had on, and directly beneath her bra. When my fingers pinched her nipple and squeezed her generous breast, I had to swallow her moan.

My mouth needed to be on her. The fact that we were in the hall didn't even register in my brain. I needed her like a fish needs water. I had tried for years to put her out of my head and my heart, but all it had taken was one afternoon and one taste to bring those teenage feelings back full force. I brought my hand out from under her shirt and unzipped her jacket. Tugging on her cami and bra, her breast spilled out in one smooth motion. She protested when I stopped kissing her, yet when my mouth latched on to her nipple and sucked, she stifled a long low moan.

I continued suckling and tonguing the tight bud as I started to pump in a constant rhythm. Her body tensed, and I could feel her fighting for a release. I ceased all movement for only a few seconds. When she started to wiggle to get me going again, I started up again hard and quick. That was all she needed. Pulling away from my feast, I covered her mouth with mine to swallow the scream I knew was coming. The girl had never been a quiet one when it came to orgasms.

As her body started to come down from the ecstasy, I could feel her muscles trembling. I fixed her shirt before helping her unwrap her legs from around me. Holding her against the wall with my hips and legs, I zipped her jacket. Avery had her hands on my waist, aiding in keeping her up, with a dreamy smile on her face. My erection strained against my jeans and I shifted, extremely uncomfortable, and more than a little wet. A cold shower and another jerking off were obviously on the line for when I got home.

"How is it you do that to me so quickly?" she finally asked, pushing on me to step back. "Wait, maybe I don't want to know."

"Your body likes my mouth," I shrugged with a smirk. "What can I say?"

"Ever the confident playboy," she teased, reaching down to stroke me over my pants.

"We should probably get back out there," I told her, feeling my eyes cross as I removed her hand and gripped it in my own. I didn't want her to know that comment bothered me, coming from her.

Making sure that all articles of clothing were straightened out, we made our way back out front. We joined the others around the stage, where they had migrated, and Chris looked more frustrated than I had seen him in a while. I had a feeling it was because of how our soundcheck had been going before we took the break.

"What's up, man?" I asked, as I released Avery and walked around to sit behind my drums, hoping to hide the bulge.

"This isn't going to work. The sound in here sucks donkey ass, and the electrical can't take all our equipment." He stated, slamming down the mic stand.

"Why don't we just do an acoustic set," I recommended. "We've done them in places like this a thousand times, and we always sound fucking awesome."

"I agree with Coop," Evan voiced, as he continued tuning his guitar. He had finished fixing his strings while we were gone.

"Me too," Matt spoke up from behind his instrument.

I could see Chris fighting with the decision, so I started a steady beat on one of my drums. Matt and Evan quickly picked up on the song and started strumming along with our hit "Our Song." Jen, Avery, and my two brothers backed up a bit and sat at the nearest table. Chris, not wanting to be upstaged, started singing the lyrics. It brought me back to our sessions in my parents' barn; some of the happiest times in my life. When the song finished, all was quiet for almost a full minute. I could see our leader working things over in his head.

"Okay," he agreed. "Let's do it."

AVERY

I *CAN DO THIS*, I thought to myself as I twirled in front of the full-length mirror on my bedroom wall.

The woman that stared back at me looked calm and collected. Her hair was done in long waves down her back and there was very little makeup on her face. The dress fell just to her knees and was a light floral print. A jean jacket and brown cowboy boots completed the ensemble, along with a few jangly bracelets and simple earrings. She looked ready for whatever the night had in store for her.

"I want to be her," I muttered, smoothing out invisible wrinkles in the fabric.

"You *are* her," Jen giggled from the doorway.

"I sure as heck don't feel like it," I told her as I scooted past her.

My stomach continued to flutter as I poked my head in to check on my father. He was sleeping peacefully and was blissfully unaware of the party being thrown tonight in his honor. He would have hated the attention, yet he would have been appreciative just the same. That was exactly how I was feeling about the whole thing.

"Are you sure you're all set?" I asked Marcia and Jeff Hall as I crossed the living room to grab my purse.

The couple had offered to stay with my dad, should he need anything, while I went down to the benefit. I felt extremely guilty, not only about leaving him, but also about causing them to miss it. They had assured me multiple times they were happy to do it.

"Yes, I went down to the bar before we came, and dropped off my stuff. The boys have done a great job," she gushed, coming over to hug us goodbye and nudge us toward the door.

The boys. I wondered if they would ever be men to her. *They were one of the reasons my stomach was doing somersaults*, I thought to myself as we made our way out to my friend's car. Well, not all of them, just a certain drummer. I don't know what I'd been thinking when I had propositioned Cooper. Who was I kidding, I knew exactly what I'd been thinking; the wisp of underwear that covered my lady parts was proof I was going ahead with it.

"What are you so nervous about?" Jen questioned, as she drove the short distance to Willie's. "You'll know pretty much everyone there."

"You know I hate being the center of attention," I reminded her. She didn't need to know about the thing with Cooper.

"It'll be fine," she said, patting my leg. "I invited Trent, so you'll have a distraction."

"I wish you hadn't done that," I groaned. "You're leading him on. I don't want to get into a relationship right now."

"He's a good man," she argued, "and maybe that's just what you need. Plus, he's a lot better than that playboy, Cooper."

I rolled my eyes at her. She had never approved of my relationship with him and when he had left me without a backward glance, it had solidified her hatred. Hence the reason I wasn't filling her in on our little arrangement. The sex was just going to be a release for the stress of my life. Nothing more.

"I'm not getting involved with Coop," I insisted as she pulled into the tavern. "But it's not fair for Trent to think he has a chance when I just don't have it in me to get involved."

"Fine, I'll back off for now," she relented, finger pointing at me. "However, as soon as your father is better, all bets are off."

Leaning over the console when she parked the car, I hugged her, hard. I knew Jen loved me and she was trying to do what she thought was best for me. Unfortunately, not everyone was meant to be happily married like her. Heck, I would settle for content. This was something I needed for me; she just wouldn't understand.

I saw Cooper's truck parked along the side of the building and that, along with the breeze teasing my legs, had me biting back a groan. I felt so exposed, yet so sexy. The secret hiding beneath my skirt gave me such a rush that if I didn't see the intended target soon, I would have to take things into my own hands.

Jen opened the door for me as I fidgeted with my outfit for the millionth time. She laughed, ushering me inside. If she only knew what was going on, she certainly wouldn't be laughing. I stood still for a moment, letting my eyes adjust, and I was floored.

We had gotten there early to help get things ready, however, they seemed to have everything under control. The band was on the stage and looked to be discussing their playlist, Willie and Rick were behind the bar, prepping, and Lexie and Maggie had some of the other early birds organizing tables and moving food. Grind Construction and "Get Well" banners were hung up, and a rather large donation jar was positioned by the entrance.

"What do ya think?" Willie asked as he approached us.

Tears filled my eyes as I launched myself at him. I was so overwhelmed with gratitude for what all these people had done for my family. My eyes squeezed shut when I felt his arms clasp tight around me. I held in the sobs that threatened to escape and took a deep breath. Feeling a little more in control of my emotions, I opened my eyes and eased up on the hold I had around my friend's neck. Before he settled me back on my feet, my gaze clashed with his brother's over his shoulder. I struggled to read his expression, but if the tick in his jaw and crossed arms were any indication, he was pissed.

Willie cupped my cheeks in his hands when he let me go, and wiped away my tears. Despite not melting into a pile of goo over this man, I couldn't help but admire the play of muscle on his forearms under all the color. Not to mention the gray t-shirt stretched across his pecs and the ball cap turned backwards, giving everyone a full view of his never-ending smile. Oh, why couldn't I have fallen for the soft-spoken sexy one?

I put my hands over his and gave him a quick squeeze before pulling away to finish mopping up my face. When he turned to hug Jen, I caught Cooper in my peripheral vision, coming our way. He looked ready to skin his brother alive. I gave him a hard look and a sharp shake of my head. What the hell was his problem?

What the hell was *my* problem? How had I thought that it could be just sex? He was the proverbial playboy, but we had a past and he had never liked to share. There was no way this would work. Especially not if he was ready to strangle his brother over a friendly hug. He didn't get to go all caveman on me. That was not how this was supposed to go.

I shifted my attention back to the man in front of me when I felt his hand on my arm. His understanding look, along with the daggers Jen was shooting Cooper had me shaking my head to clear it. Pasting a smile on my face, I hooked my arm through his and made the motion for him to show me what they had set up. While he led us to the seating area, now half-filled with tables of food, I tried to ignore the ache still burning in the same spot my barely-there underwear was covering. It would have to wait until I got home.

An hour later, I was surrounded by a couple hundred people and there was a line out the door. There had been a steady stream of local well-wishers who stopped by the table, but there were also a lot of unfamiliar faces in the tavern. I knew many of them were here to see Dark Roads, and for that, I was grateful because it took some of the attention away from us. It also kept the band busy, which meant Cooper hadn't tried to approach me again.

Suddenly a shrill whistle pierced the air. Everyone's eyes moved to the stage, and slowly they sat or quieted down. Each of the members was behind their respective instruments and Chris held his microphone, patiently waiting. My brother stood next to him, chatting with Evan.

"I'd like to say a few things before we get started tonight," Chris started. "Most of you know that we are here to show our support of one of our own, Dale Cyr, and his family. Dale has been a fixture in this town my entire life. I grew up with his kids, worked for him for a spell, and love him like a second father. When I found out about his diagnosis, it hit me hard and I knew I needed to do something. So, the band and I talked. Along with donations from the show tonight, we will be give the Cyrs a check for $20,000, to help cover medical costs."

I slapped my hands over my mouth as my eyes filled with tears. I hadn't been expecting that. Through the haze, I could see my brother wiping his face and hugging Chris; evidently, he hadn't known about it either. Keegan took the mic that was handed to him and once he had composed himself, he addressed the crowd.

"Wow, I'm speechless after that," he admitted, turning slightly toward the band to acknowledge them. "My family and I can't thank Dark Roads, and you all, enough for all of the support and love you have given us as we battle this. I'd also like to thank Willie for holding the event here. Now, without further ado, let's turn it over to the greatest group of men I know…Dark Roads!"

My brother left the stage to come back to our table, but was quickly engulfed in the throng of people. The band wasted no time jumping into one of their latest hits, and the room came alive once again. Jen bounced along with the beat in her seat next to me, and I couldn't help but smile at her.

While they played their first set, I split my time between locals and my family and friends. It was a little tiring, making small talk; however, I was happy for the distraction. I tuned out the band as best as I could and continually tried to pretend I wasn't wearing a barely-there strap of fabric under my dress.

"Come dance with me," a masculine voice whispered in my ear when the band slowed the tempo.

Tingles rode down my spine from the warm breath dancing across my skin. I turned and found Trent leaning close, his arm slung over the back of my chair. He had gradually been getting braver as the beers had flowed. I nodded, but immediately realized my mistake as he grabbed my hand in his.

When we found an empty spot on the floor, he pulled me

tightly into his arms, so we were chest to chest. His hands gripped my hips, keeping me close, and leaving me no place to put my hands except lightly on his shoulders. Trent certainly wasn't making the "friends" thing easy. The possessive way he held me signaled that, for that moment, at least, I was his.

"You've got to let me breathe, Trent," I told him, a slight teasing tone to my voice.

"I'm sorry," he apologized, letting up a bit, but still holding me close.

"No worries," I assured him as we swayed.

I felt eyes boring into me and wasn't surprised, when I glanced at the stage, to find Cooper watching us. His face was flush and the veins in his arms stood out. I couldn't tell if it was from the strain of playing or from the fact that he looked like he wanted to beat my dance partner to a pulp. I raised an eyebrow at him, as though to ask him how he had a right to be angry. He surprised me by winking and breaking into a grin. Men!

"Trent, listen," I said, leaning closer so he could hear me above the music. "You're a great guy. You're good looking, smart, nice…"

"But you aren't interested," he interrupted, flexing his hands slightly.

"No, unfortunately not," I admitted. "Not in you, not in anyone. I have too much going on right now to be in a relationship."

"Someone might want to tell the guy behind the drums that," he informed me, pulling away to kiss me on the forehead and head back to the table.

I stood there, stunned. What was he talking about? Rather than give Cooper the pleasure of looking at him again, I made my way to the bar. I needed a shot, bad. It took me a bit to reach it, as people kept stopping me and asking about my dad.

Finally, I squirmed into an empty spot and barely registered that the band had taken a break.

Leaning slightly on the counter, I signaled Rick that I wanted something when he had a chance. People nudged and pressed against me as I waited, tapping my fingernails on the top. After my drink, I was headed outside; air would be good. A few minutes later, the youngest Hall brother made his way over to me, sauntering like he owned the place, and showing a nice package tucked into tight jeans, a white Henley with the sleeves pulled up his forearms, and boots.

"What can I get you, gorgeous?" he asked.

"Two shots of whiskey," came a familiar voice from behind me.

Rick's eyebrows shot up, however, he turned to do his brother's bidding. I closed my eyes and tried not to lean back into the very male body at my back. When the shots *clinked* down in front of me, I opened my eyes and quickly grabbed one, downing it. The burn wasn't enough. While I reached for the second one, Cooper leaned closer, bringing us flush and tucking his hardened member between my butt cheeks. One hand came up to my hip to keep me against him – like I would have moved at that point – while the other found the bottom of my skirt and slid under it, to run up my leg.

Downing the shot, I banged the glass on the counter and threw Rick a smile. I moved one hand to press against Cooper's to keep it from traveling any further. I knew that with the amount of people around us and his large frame, no one could see what was happening. The thrill of it, combined with his warm, calloused hands, had my juices flowing.

Before I had a chance to say anything, I was being pulled down the hall we had been in that morning. My nipples perked at the memory and I bit my lip to stifle a moan. This time, instead of propping me against the wall, he tugged me into an office. I had made it two steps before I heard the lock *click* and my back was against the door.

"You know it's not nice to tease a man, sweetheart," Cooper growled as he undid his pants and slid them down his thighs.

The man had gone commando! Nothing covered his impressive throbbing flesh as it strained toward me. When I brought my eyes back to his, they were filled with barely restrained lust. His mouth held a smirk that said he knew what I was thinking and that he promised to uphold his end of the bargain. As much as I wanted to reach for him, I couldn't get my limbs to move an inch. When he sheathed himself with the condom from his pocket, the spell was finally broken.

"I wasn't teasing you," I panted, as he brought his hands to my thighs to lift my legs and wrap them around his waist.

"Hanging off other men?" he questioned, pressing ever so slightly at my entrance with the tip after he shifted my thong. "I don't do games. If you want sex, it's only with me."

The possessive tone in his voice nearly undid me. I strained against him and clawed at his shoulders to get him to drop me onto him. His grip on my ass tightened and he teased in and out slightly, without actually penetrating me. I moaned and found his mouth covering mine. He twirled my tongue around his and sucked gently.

"It goes both ways," I told him, pulling away and looking him in the eye. "I am not going to share your body."

"That won't be a problem," he assured me, bracing me against the door so he could bring a hand up to run it down my cheek. "I wish I could take my time, but people are going to be looking for us."

With that comment, he brought his hand back down to my ass and drove into me with one quick hard thrust. I bit down on my lip to keep from screaming out when his mouth found the spot just behind my ear and nipped. He pulled out and slammed into me again a couple of times. I could feel him getting harder and his bites soon became muffled groans in my neck. It wouldn't take much more.

Knowing his hands were occupied with holding me, I reached down to flick my clit. That was all I needed; I clamped around him and rode hard, hoping to bring him with me. His body happily obliged, filling the condom inside me with hot liquid.

My muscles started to twitch from the strain of being wrapped around him and arching into the wood behind me. I wiggled slightly and with a chuckle, Cooper helped me down. He handed me a tissue to clean myself while he disposed of the condom and got back into his jeans. I openly admired his body as he buttoned them and looked up at me.

His pants were tighter than the ones I had seen him in earlier on in the day, and they left little to the imagination. The black t-shirt he wore was equally as fitting and showed the curves of his muscled pecs. I leaned over and traced a finger up the tattoos on his left arm, leaving a trail of goose bumps on his flesh. His hand came up to stop my movements.

"I don't have time for another round, Ave," he muttered. "If you keep doing that, we are never going to make it back out there."

"Sorry," I whispered, feeling the need rise again as he ran his thumb up and down the inside of my wrist.

"Never apologize for wanting me," he said, his voice going low, "because I always want you."

"Is that why you went commando?" I asked, moving away from him to steady my nerves before we faced the crowd again.

"Yep," he laughed, flashing a genuine smile.

We were silent for a few minutes as we calmed our breathing and Cooper worked on hiding his still hard length. On his way to the door, he stopped and cupped my cheek in his hand. I leaned into it and was surprised when he dropped a soft, sweet kiss on my lips. I furrowed my brow at him, and only received a shrug of the shoulders with a slight smile in return. He reached for the knob, leaving me instantly missing his warmth.

"I'm going to go out first. Give yourself a couple minutes," he instructed. "Oh, Avery, make sure you don't have any underwear on next time."

My jaw dropped as the door clicked shut behind him. How dare he? He knew how uncomfortable I was wearing a thong as it was. No underwear, huh? Well, we'd see about that. Somehow, I needed to get control back, and I think I knew just how to do it.

COOPER

"PLEASE, COOP," SHE PLEADED, AS I slowly slid in and out of her warm folds, never fully penetrating.

I chuckled, barely holding back the load that was threatening to shoot out of my body. I wanted this moment to last forever. Avery's gorgeous wavy long hair was fanned out around her face as she tossed her head back and forth. Her eyes were glazed over in passion and her mouth was slightly open in a moan. Sweat glistened on her curvy body and she was mesmerizing.

I stilled my movements once I was sheathed to the hilt, locked inside her, relishing in what a fucking lucky man I was. The night before, when she had been coming toward me down the aisle in a flowing white dress and a loving smile, she had truly been the most beautiful I had ever seen her. This was definitely a close second. My wife, naked except her diamonds, my diamonds, my promise, wrapped around her finger, and me bare, wrapped in *her heat, as we started our life together and our own family. It didn't get any better than this.*

"Holy shit!" I gasped, jerking straight up in bed.

I dragged my hands down my face and hesitated to look beside me. The dream had felt so real that I could almost smell her. My body was still reacting from it, and my dick throbbed under the tent it was pitching in my sheets. Disappointment and surprise filled me when I confirmed that I was indeed alone in my bed.

Groaning, I rolled out of bed and padded to the master bathroom. Trying to piss wasn't even an option, I decided, when I looked down at my naked body. Instead, I leaned into the new shower and cranked the water on. Resting my shoulder on the tile outside the glass walls, I took in the room.

This was the only part of the house that was officially completed. I had removed the standard shower/tub combo and instead installed a stand-up shower large enough for two. I had also tapped into an unused hall closet to expand the space enough to accommodate an enormous claw foot tub. I had left the single vanity concept, just tweaking it so two people could use it side-by-side, if necessary. I had fallen in love with the large bowl and vintage faucet I had put in. It would be perfect for a married couple should I ever sell the house.

The thought of a married couple had Avery popping back into my head and my erection flexing against my lower abs. Letting out a soft moan, I stepped into the shower and ignored the scalding water running over my body. I grabbed my body wash and squeezed a generous amount in the palm of my hand. Bracing myself against the wall with the other hand, I started running my hand up and down my shaft with slow, even strokes, working up a lather.

My mind immediately shifted to a certain brunette and the way she had looked as I slammed into her against the door in my brother's office. She had been so hot, wet, and ready for me when I entered her in just one thrust. Increasing the strength of my grip, I started moving my hand faster. When I realized she had traded her standard bikinis in for a thong, I had almost come right there. It had only taken one finger to slide the material out of my way, so I could drive home. The memory of her pussy clamping down around me and her riding me harder in the throes of her orgasm had my hand pumping furiously to release the tingling starting in my spine. I moved the hand I had been using to hold myself up down to my balls, squeezing gently, and closing my eyes, I felt the cum explode from my body. A long low growl came with it that I couldn't hold back.

My body quivered from the exertion of my orgasm and I once again had to brace myself against the wall to keep from falling over. The now warm water soothed my aching muscles and washed off the residue. Shaking my head to clear the bewitching woman from it, I quickly washed my hair and body. When I turned the water off, I could hear banging around upstairs as the household started waking up, and the smell of bacon coming from the kitchen quickly filled my nostrils. My stomach cramped with hunger. Evidently, now that my erection was mostly gone, my stomach decided it was time to regain control.

Chuckling, I dried my body off and grabbed a pair of worn ripped jeans from the floor by my bed and a clean tank top from the top of my bureau. Once I had my boots on, I made my way out to the kitchen, whistling along to a tune playing in my head. Maybe it was time to start writing again; creating my own songs had always been something I enjoyed. Hell, our first album had been all originals. When the women and the booze had started to catch up to me, I hadn't been able to put a lick down on paper.

"Good mor…." I trailed off as I came around the corner to

the kitchen to greet Maggie and Lexie, finding them locked in a steamy embrace. "Oh man, seriously?"

Most men would be turned on by two women going at it, but for me, it was like watching my sisters, so it totally caught me off-guard. Maggie never moved from her position between Lexie's legs, while her wife did all she could to wiggle off the counter.

"Just reminding you who she belongs to, Hall," Maggie teased, finally letting Lexie down and sending her scurrying with a pinch to the behind.

"Not to mention the racket out of your room this morning, Coop, was enough to have us all needing cold showers," Evan piped up from behind me. "Did Avery sneak in after we all went to bed last night?"

"If she had, you would have needed more than a cold shower," I snarled at him, feeling my temper bubble at his mentioning her.

"I was just teasing, man," he laughed, nudging me slightly out of his way. "You know I have the utmost love and respect for your girl."

I froze, one hand on the back of my chair to pull it out. Any anger was quickly replaced with a tirade of other emotions. My girl? She hadn't been that since I had walked away from her ten years prior, but oh, didn't it sound good to hear her called that again. Did they know that we were hooking up?

I looked over at Evan, who was now filling his mug with coffee, and he threw me a wink with a knowing smile. Matt and Lexie were putting food on the table while Maggie nursed her cup, and none seemed any the wiser. Yet, Chris was leaned against the counter, waiting for his cup to be filled and was watching me like hawk. Well, it looked like the cat was out of the bag to at least two of them. Dammit.

"So, I'm going to ask you again," Chris started in as soon as everyone was seated and their plates full. "When are you coming back to Nashville?"

I had a fork full of scrambled eggs halfway to my mouth when he dropped the bomb. Looking around, I realized that they were all watching me expectantly. They had done this on purpose. It was another damn intervention. My mood immediately shifted, and I clamped my teeth together in an effort to keep my mouth shut against the things I didn't mean.

"I told you," I ground out. "I'm not sure what is going on, and that I will go when I am good and ready."

"I know what you told me," he snapped, "but we have a contract to uphold."

"Fully aware of that," I told him. "We will meet the deadline. If we don't, it won't be on me."

"We are heading back at the end of the month," he informed me, our food and the others long since forgotten as the air became thick with tension. "You. Will. Be. With. Us."

"When did you become the all-powerful Oz, dickhead?" I questioned, my hands now in fists, clenching and unclenching under the table.

"It's not just *your* dream, you fucking asshole!" he finally exploded, shoving back his chair and standing up. "It's all of ours! It's our fucking lives you're messing with."

"No shit, Sherlock," I retorted, "but it's that, and my livelihood!"

I could see a smartass remark working its way out. His eyes were dark with anger, and he was leaning toward me with his hands braced on the table. The others were quiet, but hadn't moved from their spots. They were blocking us from taking swings at each other, however I don't think they realized that it wouldn't have mattered. We would get to each other, whether they were there or not.

"I'm just getting to the point that I can handle life sober.

Hell, there are days that I want a shot so bad I can taste the alcohol," I reminded him. "I'm not ready to go back to that life yet."

"No, that's not it," he snorted. "You aren't done fucking Avery. *That's* the problem."

I saw red. I had always heard about people saying they saw colors when they experienced extreme emotions. Until that point, I had never had it happen to me. Nor had I ever blacked out without liquor.

The next thing I knew, I was straining against Evan's arms that were locked like a vise around me. Chris was bleeding from his mouth and one eye looked like it was already swelling shut. Despite the injuries, he was doing all he could to get Matt to release him. I must have gotten off a couple punches, but I couldn't recall it. The kitchen table had been shoved off to the side, along with the chairs, and the girls stood backed up against the counter, looking at us with wide, angry eyes.

"Take it back," I whispered, rage consuming me.

"No. You're thinking with your damn dick again, and to hell with the rest of us. Once you have it out of your system, you'll be ready to jump ship and come back, but it will be too fucking late."

"You ass. You know better than anyone how I feel about her," I hissed, leaning as much as I could against Evan's hold.

I saw the flicker in my band leader's eyes as he too remembered a night, not so long ago, where I opened up to him. Where I told him everything I was feeling and thinking. The worst night of coming clean, both physically and emotionally.

"Man, I've never seen anyone puke so much," Chris said, amazed, as he leaned against the bunks outside the bathroom door of our tour bus.

"I don't know how I still have anything left to come up," I replied, shivering with the chills as my stomach continued to cramp.

"*You've done good, you must be just about clean now,*" he reasoned, gingerly touching the new stitches lining his head.

"*Dude, I'm sssssooorrrrryyy,*" I told him, as my body convulsed in shivers. "*You should have just dumped me in a clinic somewhere.*"

"*I never would have done that. We're family. We will get through this together.*"

"*I appreciate that,*" I said, dragging myself up so I could lean against the cabinets and wrap myself in the blanket he handed me.

"*You would do the same for me,*" he shrugged, handing me a water as well. "*Now you can tell me what you are trying to forget with all the alcohol.*"

"*A woman, what else would it be,*" I chuckled bitterly, the bile threatening to rise again.

"*Just one?*" he joked lightly.

"*The. One.*"

"Apologize," I growled.

"Christopher, even you know that was a low blow," Lexie reasoned from her spot. "Cooper has always carried a torch for her. She isn't one of his groupies."

I could see his body relax with a sigh, and Matt cautiously released him. Still holding his hands out on either side of Chris, in case he had to grab him again, he backed up a step. Evan let up on me as well, but I could feel the heat of him at my back. He too was ready, should things escalate again. My friend approached me, hand out, blood still dripping onto his shirt.

"I'm sorry. You're right. I *do* know how you feel about her, and I shouldn't have said that."

I gripped his hand in mine and brought him against my chest, so I could pound on his back with my free hand. When I felt him return the favor, I stepped back and gave him a shove toward the living room so he could head upstairs and clean himself up. Not ready to deal with anyone else, I followed him through the kitchen and veered off and out the front door.

My legs wobbled as I tried to sit down on the stop step and as soon as I rested against the pillar, I found my hands shaking as well. Anger, confusion, and dread all surged through me. Closing my eyes, I took deep breaths and Avery's face instantly popped into my head. Only it wasn't the woman that I knew today; it was the girl I had fallen head over heels for as a rebel child. The quiet angelic brunette with the soft smile and huge heart. The one person that had always calmed me after a fight.

The adrenaline finally slowed leaving me feeling like I had been hit by a bus. Though Chris hadn't gotten any shots in, one of my hands throbbed from where it had connected with him. Stretching it a bit, I heard the door *click* and was surprised when I opened my eyes and found Maggie with a bag of ice in her hand.

"I figured you could use this," she said, tossing it to me and taking a seat against the pillar on the other side of the steps.

"Thanks," I replied, putting it against the spot that pounded along with my heart.

"You know he didn't mean that, right? What he said about Avery?"

"I do," I told her. "I also know that I am causing him a lot of stress."

"It's not all you," she assured me. "The label is panicking, and they keep getting on Lee. Shit rolls downhill, so-to-speak."

"I get it. I didn't exactly tell them where I went or when I would be back."

"No, but that's your prerogative. They might own your music, but they don't own you."

"Oh, but they think they do, and they have for the past ten years. I'm done with that. I can't live like that anymore," I admitted, putting my head in my hands.

"Sounds like you have some big decisions to make," she theorized, getting up and putting a hand on my shoulder. "Why don't you come in and let us know what the first step is going to be, so that we can help you through it."

I squeezed her hand and heard her sigh as she went back in the house. Before putting the ice back on my injury, I checked out my hand. Nothing felt broken, but it was a little swollen and red. Flexing, I felt a twinge of pain, yet nothing significant. I guess three weeks would be enough for it to heal.

Hopefully it was just a bruise, otherwise Chris would really kill me if I couldn't play. I chuckled at the thought. I was ready to finish our album. The idea of going back to Nashville for that didn't bother me one bit. Hours upon hours locked away from everyone, with just the guys and our instruments. I could handle that. The press, the paparazzi, the parties, and the questions. *That* was what I wasn't ready for.

And there was Avery. I wasn't ready to leave her yet. We had just started. Started what, I wasn't sure, but I didn't want to leave before I found out. Damn, if that woman didn't still put my head and my heart in a tizzy. I wanted to explore her body head to toe, and I wanted to be the one she turned to when she needed support through her father's illness.

Decision made, I got up and went into the house. Everyone was back around the table, plates full, trying to eat and act like nothing had just happened. Taking my spot, I smiled and accepted the juice Lexie handed me. Evan was telling a story about someone recognizing him in town and how he didn't need the band to be popular. Hardy, har, har. When he was done, I piped up.

"I'll be ready to leave with you guys at the end of the month, but it's not permanent, so you'd better be ready to work your asses off."

AVERY

"MMM," I MOANED AS A hand massaged my insole with their thumb.

"Pressure good?"

"Perfect," I whispered, leaning back and slowly feeling every other muscle in my body relax.

"Jeez, maybe we should have gotten you laid rather than a pedicure."

My eyes popped open and I turned my head to narrow them at my best friend sitting beside me. Shrugging with a slight smirk on her face, she turned her attention back to the magazine in her lap. I shook my head at her and sighed again when the woman working on my feet switched sides. Abby and Jen had decided that a girl's day was needed. I had argued very little when Jen showed up, her mother in tow. Betty Richardson had had a thing for my father for as long as I could remember, and was more than happy to be there if he needed anything for a few hours.

"There she is!" Jen exclaimed, as Abby finally came through the front door of the salon, coffee and doughnuts in hand.

"Sorry, ladies! Rough morning," she apologized, dropping her purse in a chair, along with the doughnuts, so she could hand us our coffees.

"You feeling okay?" I asked quickly, inspecting her from head to toe.

"Other than not being able to get out of my own way, I am just fine," she assured me.

Her bump was still barely there, but anyone that knew her would have to be blind not to figure out something was up. She looked so content and literally glowed. I don't know how many times I had heard that it happened with pregnant women, but I had never witnessed it until my sister-in-law. She and Keegan had finally told her mother, and from what I'd heard, she was over-the-moon excited for them. This would be her first grand-child and Abby was her only daughter, so there would be an extra level of sweetness in that.

"When are you telling Dad?" I asked, nodding at her belly as she handed us our doughnuts.

"Actually, I wanted to talk to you about that," she said, getting comfortable so the cosmetologist could get started on her pedicure. "We're thinking breakfast tomorrow morning? Just us?"

"Perfect," I told her. "He seems to do better in the morning, and gets more worn out as the day goes on."

No sooner had we made the plan did she and Jen dive in to baby talk and the fact that they were officially on vacation. I listened for a bit and chimed in here and there; but, my mind started to wander. This was the first time, outside of the benefit, that I had gotten out since my father had started his treatments. Many people had offered to stay with him, so I could run errands and such, but I had taken just a few friends up on their offers to grab groceries for me or medications from the pharmacy. I felt like he was my responsibility and I didn't want that on anyone else.

I hadn't even seen Cooper since the prior weekend. Dreams of a tattooed drummer had filled my nights on those when I actually got any sleep. Those hands, that mouth. I had woken up more than once, wet and ready for him, only to find myself alone. It was only supposed to be sex, nothing more, yet the feelings he had drawn out of me were unreachable with any other man. They were feelings I thought I had long ago buried. I would have chalked it up to lust and a dry spell, but I knew in my heart that wasn't the case.

My phone vibrated against my leg where it sat on the chair, and when I saw Cooper's name flash across the screen, my heart skipped a beat. So, it wasn't just physical. The text messages we had been exchanging that week had assured me of that. There had been a particularly long night with my father earlier in the week, and I had been tired, emotional, and ready to break. With tears streaming down my face as I sent the message, and a simple *Do you need me?* response, every wall I had erected against Cooper Hall had crumbled away.

I looked down at his new text.

C: *Getting all prettied up for me?*

A: *Well, Jen did tell me I needed to get laid*

C: *Evil woman! What did I tell you about teasing me?*

"What are you smiling about? Cooper?" Abby whispered from beside me.

I shot my head around to where Jen was sitting on my other side; however, she had moved to have her manicure done, and was engaged in a loud gossip session with a woman we had gone to school with. Letting out the breath I hadn't known I had been holding, I turned back to look at my sister-in-law. The smile on her face was that of the cat who got the canary. She knew?

"What about Cooper?" I asked cautiously, making sure I kept one eye on Jen.

"I saw him find you at the bar at the benefit, and noticed the two of you disappeared for a while," she teased. "You can't tell me nothing happened. You two stir up enough sexual tension in a room to have me wanting to drag your brother off for a quickie."

"You can't say anything to Jen," I told her, still trying to wipe the smile off my face. "Or Keegan."

"I promise," she stated with a grin, "but you gotta share some of the details, lady!"

I giggled and felt my face flush at the thought of Cooper taking me against the door in his brother's office. I was ready for more. I needed more. I wanted to take my time and inspect every muscle on his toned body, along with every piece of ink covering him.

"Yep, I need details with that face," Abby laughed.

"Oh, enough," I laughed in return, and playfully hit her on the hand.

"What did I miss?" Jen wanted to know as she heard us.

"Just girl talk," my sister-in-law answered, giving me a wink.

The rest of the day flew by. When we left the salon, I was so relaxed I thought I was going to turn to Jell-O and that the ladies were going to have to carry me home. It was a wonderful freeing feeling. I was easily coerced into a shopping trip, just as I had predicted. A new tank top and jeans were all that Abby and Jen saw, nothing spectacular, but what was hidden in the little white bag underneath them was. They were shear, hunter green, and barely there. Cooper would love them.

When we pulled up to my father's house, it was almost five and I was exhausted, yet smiling. My cheeks hurt from all the laughing and my heart felt full again. Spending the day with my best friend and my sister-in-law had been just what the doctor called for. Jen pulled to a stop behind a familiar SUV and I looked at her in question. She shrugged before giving me a hug and I climbed out of her car, waving goodbye as she pulled out of the driveway.

Abby had gone directly home from our excursion when she found out that my brother was going to be there early. They hadn't spent a lot of time together due to Keegan being so busy with work, and she was antsy for a little alone time. I couldn't blame her. I had hugged her hard and she promised to keep my secret.

I entered the house and found Marcia Hall sitting at the kitchen table with my father. The two looked to be enjoying dinner and going over paperwork. While they were occupied, I took in Dad. He had lost considerable weight with the treatments, but his body seemed to be adjusting to them and he wasn't as sick as he initially had been. They were almost halfway there, and he was holding his own.

"Hi sweetheart," he greeted, when he noticed me coming toward them.

"Hi," I returned, "what's going on?"

"Your dad messaged me and said he was up to a little work, so I brought him some of my homemade chicken soup and the Coburn file," Marcia told me. "Jeff is going to join us later for a movie."

I raised my eyebrows at my father. He gave a tired smile, yet

I could see the happiness in his eyes at spending time with some of his friends. He had always been a social butterfly and being cooped up was driving him crazy.

"Well, I'll go up and change into something more comfortable. What are we watching?"

I saw the look exchanged. "*We* are watching an action movie that the men will undoubtedly pick out. You, my lady, are going back out. Somewhere. Anywhere but here."

Again, I looked at my father. He looked at his bowl, yet I could still see the smile on his face. The plan had been his. Marcia had just been a cover. This sweet man that had always made sure my needs came before his, was doing it despite the fact that he was sick. I leaned down and gave him a hug and a kiss on the cheek.

"If you're sure?" I asked, straightening.

"Yes, and stay at the shop tonight. Don't worry about tiptoeing back in here at some ungodly hour," he told me, lightly chuckling.

I looked at Marcia for confirmation and she squeezed my hand with a smile. Leaving them so they could get back to work, I ran upstairs to pack a quick overnight bag. I stopped and gave them both kisses on the cheek, and I was on my way.

My father had converted one of the offices upstairs of the shop in to a workout room/bedroom. It had a few free weights, a bench, a bike, a treadmill, and a queen-size bed. There were times when his guys needed a place to crash and this, along with the couch in the breakroom, gave them options. As I stopped in at Claire's, I dropped Cooper a message. I don't know what I was hoping for, but I needed him to know I was alone for the night.

I got to Grind and was happy to find that no one else was around. Most of the time, the workers would borrow shop time to work on their own projects off hours. My father was fine with it, as long as tools didn't start disappearing, and they locked up behind them. Going in through the office, I locked everything behind me and had just started making my way up the stairs to the spare room with my hands full of bags, when I heard someone pounding on the door. I quickly climbed the rest of the stairs and deposited my stuff.

Before I even made it the rest of the way back down, a familiar well-built man came striding into the shop from the front offices. He stopped when he saw me, and a slow sexy smile came to his lips. The white tank top he wore showed off his tanned arms and the ink he proudly sported, while his jeans were worn, full of holes, and gripping him in ways that left nothing to the imagination. I felt my body warm and when my eyes met his, I noticed the change from light to dark, filled with unspoken promises.

"How did you get in?" I asked, when I reached the bottom stair.

"Your father still hasn't purchased a lock that can keep me out," Cooper joked, taking a couple of strides to stand directly in front of me.

With him on the floor, and me still standing on the bottom step, we were just about eye level. When his hands came up and gently cupped my face, my breath caught. Cooper brushed his lips softly over mine and our eyes locked. I was a goner. My heart was on the line and it was bound to get crushed, but damn if I didn't care anymore. I needed him like I needed air.

"Hi," he whispered, still holding my face.

"Hi," I replied, just as quietly.

Silently, I took his hand and led him back up the stairs. We had barely made it in to the room when he shut the door behind us, and turned me so my back was against it. Cooper took both of my hands in his, interlocking our fingers, and put them above our heads. I held his gaze as he brought his mouth down to mine. Caressing at first, sweet nibbles that unraveled me and caused my knees to shake, then morphing into hot, soft bites of possession that turned me wet and had my hips arching for his.

He was not to be rushed this time. His body was far enough away from mine that I couldn't rub against him. I'm not sure how long he made love to my mouth, but it was long enough that I was on the brink of having an orgasm without his hands ever touching me. When he finally pulled away to rest his forehead against mine, I swiped my eyes down his body hungrily. I could see the barely restrained tension in his muscles and the long hard length of him in his pants.

"My eyes are up here, sweetheart," he chuckled.

"Oh, I know," I told him, bringing mine back up to meet his. "I need you, Coop. Now."

"Fuck," he cursed, his mouth claiming mine once again, this time in a bruising kiss that told me his control was teetering on the line of snapping.

His hands released mine and came down to run over my hips before reaching around to cup my ass and pull me flush against him. I moaned in anticipation and hopped up to wrap my legs around his waist. Pushing against him, I ran my hands through his hair, gripping slightly. He turned us and laid me down on the bed, supporting himself with his arms on either side of my head. I let out a mewl of protest when he pulled away again.

"You aren't going to rush this, Ave," he said, reaching down to unsnap my jeans. "I am going to kiss every last part of you and remind you of what we had."

Panic started to grip my heart, but was quickly forgotten when he leaned down to place a soft kiss just below my belly button. A gentle tug and my pants were pulled down over my hips; another, and they were off. His eyes greedily took me in. I squirmed under his gaze, reaching for him when the heat became too much.

"I get to take my time tonight," he breathed, trailing more kisses down my legs from hip to toe. "Keep your hands to yourself for now."

I groaned in frustration, but did as he requested. I brought them up and gripped the pillow under my head as he continued leaving featherlike open-mouthed kisses all over my lower body. His warm breath finally stopped over the lace triangle hiding my treasure and he took me in with one suck through the material. That pressure sent me over the edge. I moaned loudly without abandon as my hands came down to hold his head. Cooper continued his skillful work until I gave him a not so gentle tug and he drew away with a chuckle, pulling the lace with him.

I braced myself up on my elbows when he stood to his full height. Reaching back over his head, he pulled his tank top off, causing his abs and arm muscles to flex in ways that would have any woman melting into a puddle of goo. His grin became cocky when he unbuttoned his pants and started to pull them down. Precum glistened at the tip of his manhood and my body ached at the sight of it. I reached for him and the smile turned soft, as did his eyes.

Coming back to the bed, he kissed his way up my stomach and I leaned back with a sigh. His hands made quick work of my tank top and my bra, his mouth never stopping. He latched onto one nipple, sucking insistently, drawing me close to orgasm again. I wrapped my legs around him, bringing us skin to skin.

"Cooper," I gasped as he switched sides of my chest. "Condom...bag by the door."

With a *pop*, he released my breast and dove for the bags I had dropped when I had gone to greet him. Pulling the box out, he made his way back to the bed, opening it as he went. When his knees hit the bed, he took one out, tossing the others aside. I grabbed it from him and opened it while he settled between my spread legs. As I ran my hands down his length to cover him, he bit back a groan and I could see him straining to hold it together.

His eyes opened as I moved my hands back above my head and he leaned down to take them in his, twining our fingers together. The quick thrust I expected never came; instead, he slid in slowly, his eyes never leaving mine. Once he was all the way in, he pulled out and did it again. The emotions on his face were more than I could take, and I closed my eyes so I couldn't see them.

"Open them, darling," he commanded, causing them to snap open. "I want to see you when we come together."

Whether it was the words or the motion of his hips, I'll never know, but at that moment, my orgasm started. I felt my insides clench around him and fought to keep my eyes on his. With a curse from deep inside, Cooper followed. We lay gazing at each other, panting for a few moments before he kissed me sweetly and moved to clean up.

There were towels by the weight bench and he made quick use of one of them before coming back to settle between my legs again. His hands brushed the hair back from my face and he watched me. All those emotions still playing across his face; love, awe, confusion, frustration were the same ones that were swirling inside of me.

Tears started to fill my eyes and I turned my head away from him. I didn't know if I could handle another broken heart from this man. My idea had been stupid from the start, and I should have known that I would end up right back where I had been ten years ago. I choked back a sob and tried to resist him when his hands worked to bring my face back to his.

"Don't cry," he pleaded. "You're killing me, Avery."

"We shouldn't have started this," I mumbled, swiping at my face. "We know how this ends. You're just going to leave again."

"I'm not going anywhere," Cooper promised, kissing the trails my tears were leaving. "You're mine, and I'm not letting that go again."

The conversation never got any further. I kissed him to keep him from saying anything else that he didn't truly mean, or promises that he couldn't really keep. I had no doubt that Cooper cared about me deeply. He said it in the way he reverently touched me, in the way he sighed when I touched him, and in the way he looked at me. However, I knew, when it came right down to it, that the band would always be his first love.

We spent the rest of the night showing our love with our bodies. When we finally drifted off to sleep, it was the best sleep I had gotten since I had been back in Maine. It was deep and void of any dreams. I was content, wrapped up in the arms of the man that I loved, and relaxed, even despite knowing my battles were only just beginning.

Slam! Crack!

"What the hell is this!" screeched a familiar voice, causing me to sit up straight in bed, my eyes going wide.

"Jen?" I questioned, gripping the sheet around me and wiping the sleep from my eyes. "What are you doing here? Is something wrong with my dad?"

Confusion and fear gripped me until I remembered that my phone was plugged in on the nightstand, and no one had tried calling me. Cooper grumbled from his spot on his stomach next to me and ran his hand down his face to wake up enough to register what was going on. Jen stood just inside the door, her hands in fists at her sides, her face turning redder by the second.

"Your dad is just fine, but you, on the other hand, have obviously lost your fucking mind," she hissed.

"What are you talking about? Why are you here?" I asked

again, now fully awake and aware that my best friend was pissed.

"I came to get you for breakfast," came her sharp retort, her arms coming up to cross in front of her chest. "What the hell is he doing here?"

"I'm not doing this with you right now," I told her. "Just go downstairs. I'll be right down, and we can go to my dad's."

"I'm not leaving until you answer me. What is *he* doing here?!"

"If you need to ask that question, I'm going to ask you how well you are taking care of your husband," I responded dryly, earning a chuckle hidden behind a cough from Cooper, who was now sitting with this legs off the edge of the bed.

He'd put himself in a less vulnerable position and had placed himself between me and Jen. Regardless of the fact that she was a woman, he wasn't going to let anything happen to me. If it hadn't been for the situation at hand, I would have kissed him and dragged him back to bed. My dig at Jen had her uncrossing her arms and taking a step closer. I saw Cooper's back tense and I put my hand out to calm him.

"I will not sit back and watch while he breaks your heart again, Avery," she said, her voice low and full of hurt. "The last time was more than I could bear."

"He's not going to break it again," I informed her, thought I was unsure of who I was trying to convince.

"I'm not going anywhere this time," he assured, reaching back for one of my hands.

"No?" she reflected, shaking her head and moving back to the door. "This time you'll rip it out and just take it with you." She turned her attention to me. "Remember what I said, Avery. This time, I won't be there to put you back together."

COOPER

Buzz. Buzz. Buzz.

Groaning, I rolled over and reached for my phone, catching a whiff of perfume on my extra pillow. Grabbing it, I moved back and inhaled deeply. The scent of cherries filled my nose and I sighed. The smell took me back to the night before and the reason I was naked beneath my sheet.

Maggie and Lexie had offered to go stay with Dale for a while, so that Avery could come have supper with me and the guys. We had made her favorite; burgers on the grill and pasta salad. When we were finished eating, we all retreated to the backyard for a bonfire. She sat down in my lap, garnering a questioning look from me, but I quickly wrapped her in my arms. The warmth from her body nestled against mine and her laughter, as the guys entertained her with stories from the road, had me getting instantly hard.

Knowing that she was limited for time, she excused us a couple hours later and led me to my bedroom. She returned the favor and took her time. The woman had kissed and caressed every inch of my body, making sure to trace her tongue and fingertips over my tattoos especially. When she took me into her mouth, I thought I was going to come off the bed. That was not something we had ever done in high school and fuck, was she good at it. Finally, when I couldn't hold it in any longer, I had maneuvered her onto her back and taken her in one hard thrust.

The guys definitely heard that one. There had been nothing I could do to quiet the long wail that came out of her mouth when I slammed into her. She had come immediately, taking me right along with her. If I was the kind of guy that got off on that sort of thing, I would have been parading around in the kitchen right this moment, banging on my chest. Unfortunately, our cuddle time had been cut short, but I kissed her, soft and sweet, to remind her that this wasn't just about sex, despite her earlier proposal. I was in it for the long run.

Now, with the smell of her all around me and my dick making a tent in the thin sheet covering the lower half of my body, I needed her. I wanted to wake up beside her every morning and wake her with me inside her. We were going to have to talk about this, sooner or later. I couldn't take too many more of these "wham bam, thank you ma'ams." Hell, when had I become a freaking softy?

Chuckling, I turned on to my back, so I could check my cell phone that kept vibrating in my hand. Propping myself up on my pillows, I saw that I had missed calls and messages from Lee and many others, enough that I had to check the time because I thought I had slept the day away. Nope, eight o'clock. What the hell?

A: *Good morning* 😊 *Wish I had woken up
with you this morning.*

That one was the only text that mattered. The one that came from Avery. The others could wait.

C: *Good morning beautiful* 😊 *I wish I
could have woken you up with me inside you.*

A: *Seriously?! That's how you respond?
Only you Coop!* 😊

C: *Just being honest, baby* 😊 *Can I
come see you later?*

A: *Of course* 💙

The heart did me in. Even though her best friend wasn't speaking to her, she had kept up seeing me and talking to me. We still hadn't finished our conversation about my not leaving her, but I had done everything in my power to show her how I felt and that I wasn't going anywhere. I had been open and honest, telling her I would have to go back to finish the album, yet letting her know it wouldn't be permanent. She had remained reserved; however, her texts and phone calls hadn't faltered.

I wasn't sure if I should go talk to Jen myself or not, but I didn't like how she had blown up at Avery. We had never gotten along, her always thinking Ave deserved better, someone more like Michael. While I didn't disagree, I wanted my chance to prove I was good enough. Evidently, she had been the one to pick up behind me and she wasn't willing to do it again. That there was another thing that Avery wouldn't talk about. Our past.

I knew I would have to leave at some point, and I didn't want her to feel alone. I wanted her to have friends she could turn to in order to combat the loneliness until I returned. I knew she had a couple of women that she worked with and kept in touch with, yet they didn't share the history that she did with Jen. I guess I knew what I needed to do. Maybe a week was enough time for her to cool down a bit.

"Dude, you need to see this!" Evan exclaimed, plowing into my room and causing me to jump a foot in the air. "Cover that damn thing up!"

"Ya know, if you had knocked like a normal person, you wouldn't be getting an eyeful of my package this morning," I told him dryly, as I pulled the sheet further up and stuck my hand out for the papers he was holding.

"Sorry," he mumbled, rubbing the back of his neck, handing me the articles, "but you're going to want to see this so you can put out some fires."

"Fires?" I asked, opening one and immediately cringing at the title.

Hall Buys House in Hometown for New Bride

"Keep looking, it gets better," he said, gesturing.

Dark Roads Permanently in the Dark?

Cooper Hall having baby with Ex, Molly Trimmer

Dark Roads replacing Hall after stay in Clover Rehab

"What the hell is this shit?!" I growled, jumping out of bed to pull on my jeans.

"They were on the porch this morning when Lexie headed out for her run," he explained, as I whipped a tank top over my head and stomped out of my room, making my way to the kitchen.

I found exactly what I knew I would when I got there. Maggie was on the phone, pissed and gesturing like a mad woman, while Matt was cooking breakfast. Lexie must have still been out running because she was nowhere to be seen, and Chris was filling coffee mugs. When he handed me mine, I nodded to him and fixed it the way I liked it before plopping down into one of the kitchen chairs with a frustrated sigh.

"You knew this was going to happen," Chris chided as he took the seat next to me. "We all did, given that we just disappeared off the grid, rather than releasing some sort of statement."

"Why the fuck do we have to answer to the public with everything that we do?" I questioned, my hands cradling my cup so tightly I was worried I might break it. "Can't our private lives be just that?"

"Unfortunately, no," Maggie reminded me, as she hung up and sat down with us. "When you signed on that dotted line, making Dark Roads more than just a high school garage band, you opened your lives to everyone."

I put my head down on the table with a *thump* and groaned. Chris was right; I had known this would happen. It always happened, but that didn't mean I had to like it. I hated the tabloids with a passion. Maggie, along with our publicist Tracey Deemer, did a lot of damage control. For the most part, we were your typical band; we liked to drink and party. We didn't get in trouble, per se. No arrests, no videos or pictures of us fighting, no bad blood with other performers. Yet, they had posted untrue stories about us for years. It was all part of the game.

"Oh shit! Avery!" I bellowed. "I need to go do damage control."

"Wait a damn minute," Chris said, pushing me back into my seat as I tried to get up. "You need to be here with us, figuring things out, before you go deal with her."

"I told you, this isn't just a booty call," I replied, pushing his hand off my shoulder. "She means more to me than that, and I'm not going to let her read those without some sort of explanation."

"Lexie is over there now, filling her in," Maggie piped up, giving Chris the stink eye. "She went over as soon as she saw those because she knew that we would be dealing with it here."

I let out a sigh and sent Chris a glare of my own. I knew he carried the weight of the band on his shoulders, but there was no reason for him to be an ass about my trying to get my life together outside of it. Matt put the pancakes he had been cooking down in the middle of the table, along with a plate of bacon, and everyone dug in. We knew we would need the fuel for the shit show that was about to happen.

After breakfast, we got to work. Evan brought me my phone while I refilled my cup, and I gave him a grateful smile. Avery was my first concern, so I dropped her a message first, telling her that I would definitely see her later to explain everything, and sent her my own heart. I knew I couldn't tell her I loved her, even though that was the first thing that came to mind. Once she had responded that we were fine and ended it with a heart, I went back to check the other messages still sitting on my phone.

Most were from other artists I was friends with, checking in; they had seen the articles and were concerned. I didn't send anything to them, as I knew that Maggie would have a general response for me to send to everyone that would cover my own ass, as well as the band's. Next, I listened to the voicemails. All but one was from Lee; basically, he called saying we needed to talk, that the band was counting on me not to fuck up, blah, blah, blah. The remaining one was from Avery and it had come in while we had been eating breakfast. Her soothing voice coming through my phone relaxed me and had the tick in my jaw easing. I didn't need alcohol when I had her, she brought me down the same way the liquor had.

Maggie and Chris moved to the living room once the kitchen was cleaned up, while Matt bailed out to grab a few things at the store – he never handled the publicity stuff very well – and Evan and I escaped to the front porch, plopping down into the rocking chairs I had recently purchased. The sky was cloudy, threatening rain, reflecting my mood perfectly. I cringed when Evan handed me the full articles to read. I didn't want to, but I figured I should know exactly what was being said about us.

The one titled **Hall Buys House in Hometown for New Bride** was exactly what the title implied. It was about me moving back to Maine to buy a house for my supposed new wife. I was floored that they listed my ex-girlfriend Molly Trimmer as the woman I had married in secret. Why were there two articles about her? We had split more than a year ago, when I'd found out that she only wanted me for my money because of her failing career. Her ability to quickly find another singer to bed confirmed that she never cared about me the way that I had cared for her.

The second one, **Dark Roads Permanently in the Dark?** was a full page write-up, questioning whether or not the band was still together. It quoted people that said we had all gone our separate ways and that we were no longer talking. They were also claiming they had seen a blowout amongst us that had ended in a couple of the guys being hospitalized. Who the hell were they getting their information from?

Cooper Hall having baby with Ex, Molly Trimmer was the one that had me fuming the most. I hadn't touched the woman since we had split. I had always been diligent about protection, and she certainly hadn't been pregnant when I last saw her, flinging back drinks at a mutual friend's Christmas party. If she was now, it sure as hell wasn't mine.

The final article, **Dark Roads replacing Hall after stay in Clover Rehab**, had my stomach churning. Part of the reason the guys hadn't dumped me at a facility was because they didn't want to feed the media more than my stupidity already had. We had tried to keep everything on the downlow, but obviously my drinking problem hadn't been as secret as I thought it had been.

Putting the magazines down in my lap, I closed my eyes and sighed. Why was all of this happening now? Just when I seemed to be getting somewhere with Avery, when I was finally at a place where I wasn't reaching for or craving a drink every time I turned around; when I had finally found peace. The whole Molly thing bothered me. Our breakup hadn't been bad, at least I hadn't thought so. I had called her out on the money thing, and she quietly slunk away, only to turn up less than a month later, wrapped around Earl Frank, an up-and-coming singer climbing the charts. We would run into each other at functions and nothing had ever been sour.

"Why do I have a feeling that Trimmer is at the center of it all?" Evan asked, after some time had passed.

"I wondered the same thing," I agreed, opening my eyes and turning to face him. "But what would she have to gain? We haven't been together in a long time."

"You know how the industry works," he chuckled. "Even stories that aren't true bring in money. Her career has totally tanked, so I'm betting she is pretty desperate."

"Why the fuck couldn't she have done this before?"

"Before what?"

"Before I started trying to convince Avery that we were meant to be together."

His eyebrows instantly shot up. I hadn't been completely

honest with the band. They knew that I was trying to get back into her good graces, but they didn't know that I planned on moving back to Maine, permanently. I wasn't sure I was ready to leave the band for good; however, I was ready to settle down a bit. Especially if it meant with her.

"Holy shit!" he exclaimed, an ear-to-ear smile filling his face. "It's about damn time you smartened up."

"Now, I just need to get her to believe me when I say I'm not going anywhere," I told him, watching carefully for his reaction.

"It's not her we need to work on, it's Chris," he reminded me. "Dark Roads isn't done yet, but that doesn't mean that we can't all have a little more personal time."

"We?"

"If you stay, I stay," he informed me nonchalantly.

"I don't need…"

"Yeah, I know, you don't need a damn babysitter," he interrupted, waving his hand. "I'm ready to come back to Maine too, and having my brother here as well just makes it that much better."

I was floored. Sure, Evan and I had been the closest in the band growing up, but I had never imagined he would move back with me. Then again, the thought of moving back to Maine permanently hadn't crossed my mind until I had seen Avery again. I thought I would just buy a house, flip it, and move back to Nashville. Evan was an only child and had spent most of his time at my house with me and my brothers, so it made sense, in a way, that he wanted to be where I was.

"Man, listen," I started, slowing my chair to a stop. "I don't want you to come back and end up being unhappy. I would feel so fucking guilty."

"Coop, I don't need a babysitter any more than you do. The choice would be mine," he said, his voice taking on a slight edge that surprised me. "You're not the only one ready for some fresh air and time away from the hubbub of city living."

"My bad," I chuckled, putting my hands up in defense. "It would be pretty awesome to have you right here, so that I can call you any time I need help on the house."

My friend's smile and laugh were quick, all tension out the window. That was one of the great things about Evan; he didn't get angry very often, and his aggravation always dissipated quickly. It was the reason I had let him stay when he met me at my front door the day I came back. With his blue eyes sparkling, he leaned over and motioned for me to do the same.

"So, how do we tell Chris that his dream for the band is about to change?"

AVERY

THE BRIGHT TABLOID COLORS TAUNTED me from across the table. I shifted on the lawn chair that I was sitting in on my father's deck, and held my mug of hot chocolate more tightly. Shivering, more from nerves than temperature, I took a sip of the hot liquid. I closed my eyes as I swallowed, and let it soothe me from the inside out. Unfortunately, when I opened them again, the magazines remained. They hadn't been just a figment of my imagination.

All I had done the night before was toss and turn. Finally, at 4:30 a.m., I gave up on any thoughts of sleep. Climbing out of bed quietly and donning a hoodie over my tank top, I'd made a drink to calm my nerves and decided it was time for a little reflection. The next few hours were mine before I had to take my father in for treatment.

Lexie had been amazing when she had shown up days before, with all the articles in hand. She explained everything to me in detail, including the situation with Molly and the fact that the pictures were a couple of years old. Cooper couldn't even take credit for her coming over; it seems she had taken it upon herself. That group was a well-oiled machine when it came to this kind of stuff, and fiercely protective of those around them.

I sighed as I zeroed in on the article that bothered me the most. ***Cooper Hall having baby with Ex, Molly Trimmer***. The others were merely annoyances, but this one struck me to the core. Marriage and relationship rumors were forever buzzing around celebrities of all kinds, it was expected. Yet, the idea of Cooper having a child with another woman made my heart ache, and took me back to how I felt when he walked out on me at eighteen.

"I thought I told you to burn those damn things," came a whispered growl from the doorway, that nearly sent me backwards in my chair.

I placed the mug down on the table before I could spill anything on me, and turned to look at the man who had been racing through my mind. Cooper came over the night before to talk. While he trusted Lexie with everything in him, he had wanted to assure me himself. The talking hadn't lasted long. My need to feel him, touch him, and show him how I felt, took over.

He padded over to me, barefoot, in his worn work jeans that were full of holes, and wearing a Dark Roads tour shirt from a few years ago. His hair was spiked from me running my hands through it and he scratched at his beard when he drew near enough to see the one that I was looking at. Eyes narrowed, he pulled out the chair next to me, and turned it so that when we sat, we were knee to knee.

"Avery, we talked about this," he said quietly, taking my hands in his as he rested his elbows on his knees.

"I know we did, but that doesn't make them go away."

"I understand that," he replied. "However, you have to trust me here."

"I get this is part of your life," I stated slowly. "You have to remember though, it's not part of mine."

His brown eyes met mine and I saw emotions flicker through them so fast that I couldn't keep up. I knew this couldn't be easy for him because it seemed he truly was trying to change his life. But how was I supposed to completely trust someone I thought had loved me, that had walked away without looking back? My heart and my head were so conflicted. It hadn't helped when the actual magazines showed up on my doorstep the day before, so I knew that Jen was putting in her two cents.

"Baby, I'm sorry," he apologized. "None of those are true. I'll tell you as many times as you need to hear it. I'm also not going anywhere. Maine is going to be my home base again."

"You have to go back to Nashville. Who's to say that you aren't going to go back, find another girl to warm your bed, and decide that you missed being there?"

Letting go of my hands, Cooper sat back in the chair in frustration. He covered his face and let out a groan before dragging his hands down and setting them in his lap. The hurt showed in his face. The night before, I had alternated between holding him as close as I could, not wanting to let go, and rolling over to put my back to him. When the time came that he normally would have left – I was still pretending my father didn't know about us – I had wrapped myself around him and asked him to stay.

"That's not going to happen," he argued. "Everything I want is here. *You* are here."

"It didn't stop you before," I snapped, quickly slapping my hand over my mouth.

"You're right," he agreed, "it didn't. Now is different. I'm older and, I'd like to think, a little wiser."

He shifted his chair back slightly and moved as though he was going to get up. Feeling like a piece of crap for having let my fear turn me into a bitch, I got up and curled myself up in his lap. His arms came around me without hesitation and he kissed my forehead.

"I'm sorry."

"Don't be. I was an asshole when I was a kid. If you had been smart, you would have never taken up with the likes of me, or you would have moved on to some business man that could run circles around me," he muttered.

"No one ever said I was smart," I joked lightly.

"You are, and before you realize that you can do better, I'm going to head home," he told me, squeezing me tight and kissing me on the head one more time before helping me to my feet.

"You never give yourself enough credit, Coop."

"We all have our things," he reminded me, cupping my face in his hands.

I leaned into him when he moved to kiss me. It was meant to be a mere brushing of lips; however I tugged at his belt loops to bring him close, and I took it deeper. I knew he only needed to hear a little moan from me and he would take control of the situation. Doing just that, his hands slid from my face down my arms and ribs, to move around and cup my ass through my shorts and bring my hips flush against his. As his tongue dueled with mine, I slid my hands under his shirt and scraped my nails against his abs and up to his pecs. This time, it was his turn to make a noise and I smiled when he pulled away, hissing.

"Your dad is going to be up soon, and I need to get out of here before he does," he said, his voice low, forehead pressing against mine.

"It's too late for that, Hall," was my dad's retort from behind him, causing us both to jump. "Why don't you stay for coffee?"

"Morning, um, sir," he replied, turning slightly to nod to him. "I should probably head home and make sure the rest of the band didn't burn my house down while I was gone."

The excuse was a weak one, but it made both my father and I smile. With a slight wave, my dad turned, and I could hear him shuffle to the counter to make his cup of tea and some toast. With less than two weeks left to go in his treatments, he still didn't have much of an appetite, yet he was very good about eating a least a little something before we headed to the hospital.

"Since I now feel like a teenager caught making out on the living room couch," Cooper muttered, "I'm going to head out."

Kissing me quickly on the lips before I could grab him again, he turned and headed into the house. I laughed at his retreating form and moved to pick up my mug. The hot chocolate was still slightly warm, so I drank it without looking at the table.

"Come sit with me," my father requested softly. I jumped at the sound of his voice. I hadn't realized that I had been staring off into space for a while.

I sat back down in the chair and shuffled the magazines into a pile. I liked to think my father was oblivious as to what was going on, especially since he was dealing with his illness. However, when his hand came down on mine to still my movements, I knew otherwise.

"Talk to me, girl," he pleaded.

"Everything is fine, Dad," I told him. "I promise."

"That's bull, and we both know it," he scoffed. "This stupid pile of horseshit has you second-guessing Cooper."

"That came ten years ago when he walked away, not from these articles."

"I could have wrung his little neck back then," my father chuckled.

"You're laughing about the fact that his leaving left me depressed and withdrawn?" I asked in disbelief.

"No, girl," he admonished. "I'm laughing because he is every bit the young man that I was. Always had a feeling of lacking and like I needed to prove something. I never felt good enough for your mother."

"Only to find out you deserved better," I reminded him. "You turned into a pretty amazing man."

"You may be partial," he winked, leaning over to cover my hands with one of his again. "Cooper is trying to do the same thing."

"How can you be so sure? Just because he says so?"

"A man's word is a strong thing," he said, squeezing my hands before releasing them and taking a sip of his tea. "But it only means as much as the actions behind it."

"Dad, how am I supposed to believe him when these things pop up? After everything that happened years ago?"

"You need to let go of the past and look forward. Neither of you is the same person; you've both grown up."

"Has he?"

"Who turned you into such a cynic?" he asked, amazed.

"Cooper," I laughed, the irony of it all not lost on me.

"You're getting a second chance with him. Do you really want to give that up without knowing what could happen?"

With that wisdom, my father pushed himself up from the table. Before grabbing his cup and plate, he picked up the magazines and tossed them into the fire pit just off to the side of the deck. My eyebrows shot up at his actions, but he just kissed me on the top of the head and took his stuff into the house.

"Oh, and Ave," he commented, sticking his head back out

before I got up. "Send Jen a message and let her know that she can keep her garbage next time."

I giggled, like a little girl, the way I always had when my dad made one of his dry, sarcastic comments. Even though he was sick, he was still my father. Doing just as he asked, I snapped a picture of the fire pit and sent it to Jen with a simple request. I knew her thoughts, and I didn't need hers interfering with mine.

An hour later, we were both cleaned up and on the road. We weren't due at the hospital for my father's treatment for another hour; however, we had a stop to make. Over the last four and a half weeks, we had come up with a routine. At the beginning of the week, before dad was too worn out from his sessions, we would stop at the closest Grind job sight, so he could check it out. That, along with learning of Abby's pregnancy, seemed to help lift his spirits.

Pulling up to the warehouse the guys were working on in the next town over, I was pleasantly surprised to see both Keegan and Rick on site. The two of them were leaning on the hood of my brother's company truck, looking at plans while the crew was at work framing. My father jumped out of my car before I could even pull it to a complete stop. I smiled at his excitement and the look on his face. He was completely content.

I turned off my car and leaned on it as I watched the three men interact. The two moved apart so that my dad could step up between them and see what they were looking at. My brother threw me a smile as my father prattled on and pointed out items on the blue print. This was one thing I dearly missed, while living in Massachusetts. I didn't get to see this interaction, the kind that made my heart full.

"He looks good." Rick's low voice next to me startled me.

"He does," I smiled.

"He's happy to have you here, despite the circumstances," he told me, nudging me with his shoulder.

I nudged him back and took in my father. Even though he had been undergoing aggressive treatments that left him sick and tired a majority of the time, he looked good. He was pale, sure, but his cheeks held a slight pink tinge this morning and his smile was never-ending. The weight would come back later. It was obvious the fight was still in him.

"I hope so, Rick. I really hope so."

"He is, darling," he assured me. "As are a few others."

The wink he threw me caused me to laugh. The Hall brothers were definite charmers, and I had missed them. All of them. I had grown up with them, just as I had with my own brother. I looped my arm through his and laid my head on his shoulder. He covered my hand with his, and gave it a squeeze.

"In all seriousness, Avery," he whispered. "We've all missed you. Cooper or not, we'd all like to see more of you."

The sadness in his voice had me lifting my head and looking into his blue eyes. The fitted ball cap he wore backwards kept the too-long hair out of his face, so his gaze easily locked with mine. There was no sexual innuendo this time, no joking around. Then it hit me: when I had bailed out of Maine to escape the memory of Cooper, I had also left people that loved me. I had done the same thing to them that he had done to me.

My chest suddenly felt heavy and my eyes filled. I looked over to where my brother was still reviewing plans with our father. He sensed my gaze and this time, his smile was different. It was warm, soft, and full of love. I knew I had missed him, but Rick had just solidified everything I had been questioning. Cooper wasn't the deciding factor.

"Maybe it's time I moved back home," I told Rick, squeezing his arm and settling my head against his shoulder once again.

COOPER

E VERY POSSIBLE SCENARIO OF WHAT could happen played through my mind. I knew she would be angry; hell, I was pissed with myself for not telling her sooner. We had known for a while when we were flying out, I had just been too damn chicken to tell her. Would she stop talking to me again? Would she end whatever it was we had started?

I had less than a week to figure it out. I had six days to tell her we were leaving for two months to finish our album...six days to convince her I was coming back. I wasn't ready to give up on Avery yet. I would do everything in my power to show her what we had was special and that I would be there for her. I was going to have my music and her as well.

Sighing, I adjusted the Patriots hat I wore to keep the sun

out of my eyes and gave the lawnmower a little more throttle. I had bought an old John Deere riding tractor from my father so I had something to mow with, and helped to fund the upgrade he had been dreaming about. I didn't mind that the tractor had been new when we were teenagers. My father had taken good care of it and it still purred like a kitten when it started.

Between Nashville and touring, I had forgotten how relaxing the little things could be. The demo and reconstruction on the house, acoustic sets out by the campfire, and mowing the lawn. To many, they would feel like work, but after being cooped up on a tour bus or stuck in a studio for hours on end, they felt like a breath of fresh air. They calmed the last of my frayed nerves.

Well, they did until I saw a Grind truck pull down the long drive with Keegan at the wheel. I tried to gauge his mood as he drove toward me. I was able to let out the breath I hadn't realized I had been holding when I noticed that his window was rolled down and he was grinning. Dale was fine, otherwise he would have had a much different look about him. I smiled back and stopped the mower where I was. Just as I turned it off, he pulled up next to me.

"Man, the house looks fucking amazing!" he exclaimed, climbing out and gesturing to the building.

"Thanks, Keeg," I replied, shifting slightly in my seat. "It's still a work in progress, but we are moving along."

"You have done a lot already," he noted, leaning on the hood of his truck. "I can't wait to see it when you're finished."

"I'll have a housewarming party when it's complete," I told him, getting up and stretching my legs.

While his stance said he was easygoing and here for a friendly visit, I knew by the look in his eyes that wasn't the case. Keegan had taken my brothers and I under his wing when we were kids. He never changed his attitude when Avery and I had become a couple, yet there had been an unspoken agreement between us. I was damn lucky he hadn't laid me out flat when I had first returned home, and I knew that.

"I know you can appreciate what I'm doing with my house, man," I said, widening my stance a bit and crossing my arms over my chest, "but I also know that's not why you are really here."

"Not one to beat around the bush, are you?" he asked, coughing around a chuckle.

"We've known each other too long for that, Cyr," I reminded him.

"True. Long enough for you to know that I love my baby sister," he stated.

There it was. The real reason he had pulled in, in the middle of a weekend afternoon at a time I knew Avery was off shopping with his wife while my father was hanging out with Dale. He had been smart enough to come have a man-to-man chat with me when he knew that he wouldn't get caught.

"I'm fully aware." I nodded.

"You broke her heart the last time, Hall," he recapped, an edge creeping in to his voice. "You walked away without looking back, and I watched my sister turn in to someone I didn't even know."

"I know."

"Do you? Do you know that I held her while she cried herself to sleep more nights than I could count? Do you know that I hid everything I could from my father, so he didn't run to Nashville to kill you? Do you know that I wanted to turn your brother away when he came looking for a job, just because of what you had done?"

The cracking of his voice and the clenching of his hands had me turning my head. I couldn't look at him. This was one of the strongest men that I knew, behind his father, and I had caused him anguish. My heart broke, not only for what I had done to Avery, but for what I had done to him. Never mind the fact that I had almost cost my youngest brother his dream job without even realizing it.

Anger was no longer the first emotion to take over when I thought about the decisions I had made. Now, pain filled me. When Keegan gripped my forearm, I turned slowly. If he hit me, I wouldn't hit him back. I deserved it. Hell, he should have done it a long time ago.

"Cooper, look at me," he requested, his voice a little clearer. "Promise me you won't do it again. I can't handle holding her together *and* dealing with my dad's illness."

"I'll tell you the same thing I have told her," I said, reaching out to grasp his shoulder with my free hand. "Maine is my home base again and as long as she is here, I'll be here."

The relief in his face was immediate. Emotions were flowing high and I almost fucking lost it when he pulled me into a crushing bear hug. He not only loved his family above all else, he was worn out. I couldn't imagine what he was going through, juggling it all. Between his father, the business, and a new baby on the way, he had to be overwhelmed.

"Sorry, man," he apologized, pulling back and hastily wiping his face.

"Don't be, Keeg." I shook my head. "I'm here for you and your family, regardless of what happens with me and Ave."

"Just know that if you do take off, I will hunt you down," he said, a ghost of a smile on his face, the edge back in his voice.

"Duly noted," I told him, shaking his hand before he turned to get back in his truck.

"Ya know, Coop. Knowing your history, I never would have picked you for my sister, but at the same time, I don't think I could have picked anyone better."

Despite the craziness of the statement, I knew exactly what he meant. I nodded, pulling on my brim slightly as he waved, turned around in the driveway, and headed out. Not wanting any of the guys to come out and ask what was going on, I jumped back on the mower and got to work.

Once the lawn was finished, I moved on to weed whacking, my mind still racing from my encounter with Keegan, my chest was still tight. I had known we would eventually need to talk, I just hadn't realized the weight he carried around. The selfishness of my eighteen-year-old self was kicking my adult self in the ass.

I was just finishing around the back of the house near our fire pit when I heard a motorcycle pull into the driveway. Only one person I knew drove one and he had yet to step foot on my property since I had been home. Sure enough, when I came around the corner, Willie was coming to a stop and turning off his Harley. Taking my time, I put the trimmer in the storage shed and followed him with my eyes as he climbed off and removed his helmet.

Growing up, Rick and I had always been closer. I wasn't sure if it was the middle child thing or what, but Will had always kept to himself. Our relationship only became more strained when Avery and I became involved. Everyone had joked that it was because he was jealous and had a crush on her. I had laughed about it then, yet with the way he had acted since I'd been home, I had a feeling they hadn't been far off from the truth.

"'Bout time you came to visit," I joked lightly, moving to sit on the porch steps.

"I see your twang is finally gone," he shot back, a lift to one corner of his mouth.

I shook my head with a chuckle, feeling some of the earlier stress ease. Taking digs at each other was the norm for us, and the familiarity felt good. While he came over to lean against the post across from me, I stretched and continued to watch him.

The light-hearted joking was a front, I soon noticed. He immediately crossed his arms when he got comfortable and the smile he gave me held no warmth. I quickly went through the last couple of days to see if I could remember doing anything to piss him off. Nothing came to mind.

"So, what brings you to my humble abode?" I asked, mimicking his stance from where I sat.

"I thought it was about time we had a talk," he informed me, muscles tightening under his ribbed tank top.

"You didn't come for the grand tour?" I teased, hoping to keep things lighter than my conversation with Keegan. A single deep one in a day was more than enough for me.

"Not today," he replied, never batting an eyelash.

"Fine," I said. "What is this about?"

"Avery."

I hadn't had to ask to know that was coming. His eyes bore down on me, begging to give him a reason to hit me. I saw his fists flex slightly when I bent my leg. He was out of luck today. All the fight had finally left me.

"What about her?"

"That's exactly it!" he fumed. "You treat this thing with her like a big joke."

"What the hell are you talking about?" I questioned. Either he was jumping ahead of himself, or I had totally missed something.

"You sleep with everyone under the sun and have absolutely no regard to anyone's feelings," he forged on. "Women are just notches in your freaking bed post."

"That's not true—"

"I'm not done," he cut me off, his face turning reddening as he went on. "Just because you're some big-time country star doesn't give you the right to come back into town, hook up with an old flame, and tarnish her reputation. We could all figure out that you had the biggest set of balls in the Hall family, without you having to be an asshole about it."

I shook my head when his rant finally ended. It was more than about Avery; I knew that and so did he. Looking up at him, I was seriously worried he was going to have a heart attack. All of his muscles were straining, and his breathing was quick. My guess was that the magazines had tipped the iceberg with him. Everything had been building up for some time, and they just sent him over the edge. Not really wanting to come to blows with my brother, yet willing to defend myself against untrue allegations, I treaded lightly.

"I'm not going to argue with you that I was a dumb fuck for leaving her the way I did, or try to justify what I've done on the road the last ten years," I started.

"You could have had your pick of women in town, Coop," Willie interjected. "Why her again? She was finally getting over you."

And she's finally available for me. He hadn't finished the sentence with that phrase, but he might as well have. It was unspoken, yet implied loud and clear. His crush had obviously been so much more than that. I wondered if she realized how easily she could have the "better" brother. One that wouldn't have caused her all the heartache.

"Because I love her, and I think I deserve a second chance," I told him, quietly, simply.

"You deserve it?" he snorted. "You've got everything else you've ever dreamed of. Couldn't you have let one of us get something?"

Ding! There was the green-eyed monster, rearing its ugly head. I racked my brain quickly to remember what he had wanted to be when he grew up. I couldn't come up with anything, though I'm sure bar owner hadn't exactly been on his list. It still surprised me to hear the venom in his voice. If anything, I was jealous of him – the fact that he had a "normal" life, and that he was a business owner. That alone was no easy feat.

"You think sleeping in a 1985 Winnebago with six other guys, traveling city to city, and having food and who knows what else thrown at you, is glamorous? You think being so tired you can't make it to your bed, never mind trying to call loved ones because of the time difference, fun? You think living in a 5,000-square foot home with paparazzi just outside the gates is wonderful? It gets pretty lonely and exhausting, let me tell you."

"Yeah, you looked lonely," he sputtered, a little anger reseeding.

"The magazines aren't all truth, you know," I reminded him as I stood.

"No shit," he muttered, "but proof is in the pictures."

I rolled my eyes before I could catch myself. Old habits die hard when you're bickering with your sibling. His hands immediately clenched again and his back straightened. Clearly, nothing I said was going to change his mind.

"That's exactly what I'm talking about," he repeated, pointing at me. "You don't take anything seriously."

"I'm sick of defending myself to everyone when their minds are already made up about me," I huffed. "You're beyond listening at this point. It's just going in one ear and out the other."

In front of my eyes, Willie's face seemed to get redder, if that was possible. Evidently my pointing out the obvious wasn't the best move, but I'd had enough. We were getting nowhere, other than listing out the things I'd done wrong with my life.

"I love Avery, and I'm going to do my damnedest to show her that. I'm not going anywhere. Maine is my home base from now on," I informed him, feeling like a broken record, crossing my arms in front of my chest. "You should have gone after her when you had the fucking chance."

I knew that last sentence was a mistake the moment it left my mouth. I deserved what I had coming, for that one. I didn't bother to move to avoid or soften the blow when my brother's fist shot out. Maybe one punch would make him feel better.

It had been a long time since I had been in a brawl of any kind. Long enough that I forgot how it felt. Will hadn't held anything back. The force and the pain exploding in my face brought me to my knees. My hands flew to my face trying to stop the blood gushing from my nose. I hadn't heard it crack, so I could only hope it wasn't broken, but I would have two killer black eyes by morning.

Just as he started to reach for me, anger flashing in his eyes, the guys came running out of the house. Matt and Chris each locked onto one of his arms as Evan came over to help me up, handing me a rag in the process. I swayed when I stood to my full height, and my buddy reached out an arm to steady me. I shook him off and leaned slightly on the deck. I closed my eyes as I gingerly pinched and moved my nose around. Nothing was broken, though it hurt like hell.

When I opened them again, the guys still held my brother, who seemed to finally be calming down. His face now held a little remorse for what he had done, and he nodded his head when Chris asked him if he could let go. Will rubbed his hands down his face and eventually looked up at me, apologizing with his eyes. I nodded and put my hand up to keep him from saying anything.

Before a word was uttered, a red Grind truck came down the driveway. Rick had Luke Combs blasting from the speakers, and seemed oblivious to the activity on the porch as he pulled to a stop behind my Dodge. He hopped out, whistling along to the music, as he opened the passenger door to grab the five large pizzas we had ordered from Claire's for supper. When he got to the steps, he stopped, startled by all of us standing there, me still holding the blood-soaked cloth to my face.

"What the hell?" he mumbled.

"Just get up here," I muttered around the rag. "I'm freaking hungry."

He stumbled up the steps, his eyes dancing between me and Will. I pushed off the railing and went to the door, holding it open with my foot, and gestured for everyone to head inside. Evan led the way, a grin on his face. Rick followed, with Chris and Matt hot on his heels. Will stood right where they had left him, looking from his bike to the door, like he wasn't sure which way to go.

"Come on, you asshole," I said, leaning a bit to take him by the arm. "Let's go eat."

AVERY

THIS WAS IT, I THOUGHT to myself as I pulled off the interstate and onto the main drag that would take me back to Lane & Son Management Co. I had only been gone nine weeks, but it felt like forever. Weirder still was that I didn't feel like I was coming home; I felt like I was just a visitor. The decision had been made.

I sang along to Reba McEntire's "Fancy" as I stopped at a red light and rolled down my window. The day was starting to warm up, but I didn't want to turn on the air conditioner just yet. The fresh air calmed my nerves as I accelerated with the green light. To say I was nervous was an understatement. Julie wouldn't be happy that I was going back to Maine, but she would understand.

I was also a little jittery about leaving my father. I had been the one taking him to treatments, so I was feeling a little guilty that I had left so someone else had to take him. Abby had been more than happy to spend the day with him when I approached her. She was feeling better than in the earlier weeks of her pregnancy and my dad got a twinkle in his eye whenever she was around. He couldn't wait to be a grandfather.

As I signaled and pulled into the parking lot of the building I had worked in the for the last few years, a million and one emotions bombarded me. Moving away had been what I had thought I had needed all those years ago; however, I was now realizing it had probably only made matters worse. Either way, Julie had been an incredible employer and friend. That was one thing I didn't regret about my move south.

Getting out of the car, I smoothed my slacks and the flowing tank top I had put on. Reaching back into the vehicle for my work bags, I sighed. I loved my job, and I didn't want to give that up; however, I didn't believe that Julie wanted a ghost employee. Dad had assured me that Marcia could use my help at the office, or Keegan, out in the field. I told him I would figure everything out when he was back on his feet.

"Hi, Kelly," I greeted the receptionist as I entered the lobby.

"Welcome back, Avery!" she responded. "Julie is ready when you are."

"Just let her know that I'll put my stuff in my office and be right down."

She nodded and picked up her phone to relay the message. I headed to my office and was surprised to find the door open. Kelly had obviously prepped for my arrival. Fresh flowers filled a small vase on the conference table, all spaces had been dusted, and the windows were open a crack, letting in the late-June breeze. My heart warmed at her thoughtfulness, and I chuckled knowing Julie was probably having a fit because windows open meant the air conditioning system for the building would run more. It had been a longstanding battle between the two of us.

Setting everything down, I removed a file from the bag and turned to make my way to Julie's office. Her door was open as well and she was perched on the couch, papers surrounding her. Her black heels had already been discarded near the coffee table and her bare feet were tucked up under her body as she read over a file in her hand. Her black slacks and purple shirt were wrinkle-free and ever professional, along with the long brown hair that was wrapped in a French twist. It was hard to believe five years separated us.

"Are you going to keep staring or are you going to shut the door and sit down?" she asked, breaking me from my reverie.

"Sorry," I mumbled.

Turning to do as she requested, I shook my head to clear it. I was coming to realize how much I was going to miss her and our friendship. She was one hell of a businesswoman, and knew how to run her company. I admired her.

"How's your dad doing?" she questioned, reaching out for my arm when I settled on the couch beside her.

"He has his good days and his bad days," I told her, relaxing a little under her touch. "Just one more week left of treatments."

"He'll come out of this stronger than ever," she assured me, pulling her hand back into her lap.

"I hope so," I replied, handing her the folder I held. "Either way, it's time for me to go home."

Her face was void of emotion as she opened it and found my resignation letter. Without a word, she put the folder on the table and grabbed one of her own. Handing it to me, she sat back with a smile. I raised an eyebrow at her, but she shook her head and nodded at the paperwork in my hands.

Upon opening it, I found a stack of legal jargon. I skimmed a little bit and saw the words, "partnership" and "Maine."

Confused, I looked at her and saw that her smile had increased significantly in wattage.

"Lane & Son is expanding into Maine," she informed me, "and I want you to run that division."

"What?!" I exclaimed, nearly dropping the file in my haste to hug her.

"It won't be brick and mortar for a while; however, we have four companies in the state already lined up and ready to work with us," she explained when I sat back again.

"But, why now?"

"It's time," she replied. "I'm not ready to lose you, and I can't be in two places at once."

"A partnership, though?" I wondered.

"I know financially you can't afford it, but that's where this is headed. For now, I will make you CFO. Your pay will increase, as will your responsibilities."

"Julie…"

"I know you have a lot going on with your dad," she said, cutting me off. "We will work around that."

I couldn't believe it. I was the senior-most member of Julie's staff, but I hadn't seen this coming. I knew the company prided itself with having a member of the family as an owner. I wasn't sure what I had done to earn it, but I wasn't going to argue with it. It was my dream, owning a company and doing what I loved.

"I'm not family," I reminded her.

"You are to me," she said simply. "I'm an only child with no kids. This company needs to live on, and it will take two of us to make that happen. My father was thrilled when I mentioned you."

"Okay," I caved. "I'm in. What do we do now?"

We spent the rest of the day signing paperwork, going through files, and reviewing what came with the CFO position. When I stepped out of the building with the last box from my office, I stopped short. We had been in and out all day, transferring files to my car that would come with me, but I hadn't realized how late it had gotten. The intent had been to return to Maine that night, but I still needed to pack up what I could at my house here, so they could rent it out again. It had been such a whirlwind of a day that I hadn't even called home to let everyone know what was going on. I would have to do that when I got back to the house.

My brain was still spinning as I made the short trek. It was going to be weird not being at this office any more, however Julie assured me that we would have one set up in Maine as soon as cash flow permitted. She was even willing to do it close to me, so I didn't have to do much traveling. It was so surreal. Maybe I'd check with Keegan to see if Grind was working on any new office buildings close to home.

"*Ooof!*" I gasped as I slammed on my breaks.

I had been so distracted when I pulled into my driveway that I hadn't noticed the pickup parked in my spot. Cooper's Dodge filled the space my car normally occupied, unsure what was going on, I turned off my car. The house was lit up and I could see his shadow behind the blinds in my bedroom.

"What is he up to?" I whispered to myself as I made my way up the walkway and into the house.

'90s country blared from my living room stereo. There I found boxes everywhere, filled in varying states, and I could hear Cooper's deep voice singing along from upstairs. My lips parted in a content smile, and I took the stairs two at a time to get to him. When I reached the doorway of the bedroom, I leaned against it and took him in. He was wearing worn jeans that cupped his ass where he was squatting in my closet, putting shoes into a box, his black tank top stretched taut over his shoulder muscles, and his cowboy boots molded to his feet. The man was eye candy, and after not having seen him for the last five days, I was ready for a piece.

I was just starting to move toward him when he turned and stood. I stopped dead in my tracks and squeaked in surprise when I saw his face. My noise caught his attention and he smiled broadly when he saw me. I rushed to him and gently cupped his face in my hands, while his dropped the box and landed on my hips. Cooper's nose was slightly swollen, with a cut across the bridge. That wasn't what had shocked me; it was the two black eyes he had.

"What the hell happened?" I cried, running my hands along the planes of his face, searching for other injuries.

"Just a little misunderstanding with my brother," he chuckled, pulling my body tighter against his. "Nothing a little love from my lady can't fix."

I couldn't ask any other questions because his mouth devoured mine then. Clearly, I hadn't been the only one missing something. His teeth nipped at my lip, seeking entrance, and I sighed, allowing his tongue to reach in and touch mine. What I thought was going to be a duel of wills and wild passionate sex, actually turned into soft caresses and reverent lovemaking. Neither of us wanted to miss a moment. Something had changed.

After removing my clothes and planting soft open-mouthed kisses over each part of my body as he revealed them, he lifted me under the butt cheeks and wrapped my legs around his hips. The cotton of his jeans rubbed against my bare clit and I nearly came undone when he moved to lay me back on the bed. I watched him as he pulled his shirt off over his head, muscles rippling, tattoos dancing on his arms. Unable to resist leaning down to kiss me, he leaned one knee on the bed and brushed his lips against mine while he undid his pants.

When he finally joined me back on the bed with a condom

in hand, I took it from him. Opening it, I rolled it down the hard shaft that strained toward me begging for release. Cooper wasted no time in sheathing himself inside me once we were protected. I wrapped my legs around him, once again pulling him close, and reached up to lock my hands with his. He rocked against me in a slow steady rhythm that hit my sweet spot every time. I purred my approval, never letting my eyes leave his, even when they nearly closed in ecstasy.

I sensed my orgasm building and tried my hardest to hold it at bay. Everything felt so good and I didn't want it to end. Cooper must have noticed my body starting to clench around him because he stopped moving. Locked inside me, he leaned down and placed gentle, sweet kisses on my forehead, cheeks, and lips. Finally gripping my hands tightly in his and leaning his forehead against mine, I could feel him pulsing inside me.

"Avery, I love you," he whispered, his voice cracking with emotion.

"I love you, too, Cooper," I moaned, as he shifted his hips and the pressure on my clit took me over the edge.

He followed me seconds later. As we came down from our high, he pulled out of me and climbed out of bed to dispose of the condom. Cooper quickly returned, pulling me to him and wrapping me in his arms. I laid my head against his chest and took in the steady beating of his heart. It nearly put me to sleep, when my eyes shot open.

"Wait, did you tell me that you loved me?" I asked, propping myself up on his chest to look at him.

"Took you long enough," he chuckled, tucking a lock of hair behind my ear with a finger.

"Do you really?" I asked, my voice low.

"Always have," he answered, "and always will."

I climbed up to straddle him and gave him a long, slow kiss. This man. He would be the death of me. I had loved him once, and it broke me in ways I couldn't have imagined. What if it happened again? Could my adult heart handle it better than my teenage one had?

"Stop overthinking," he told me, tapping me affectionately on the nose.

I giggled and squirmed against him as he maneuvered us so he was once again on top of me. A wide grin split his handsome face when he reached under the covers to tickle me lightly across my ribs. He might break my heart again, but he made me smile. He was who I was meant for. Kissing me hard on the lips, he swatted at the side of my butt and climbed out of bed. I rolled over on my side to watch him as he pulled on his jeans.

"Where are you going?"

"I brought Chinese food," he said, leaning down to kiss me again. "Get dressed and come downstairs."

"Such a man," I mumbled to his retreating form, earning myself a laugh. "Sex and food, that's all that matters to you."

I dug around in drawers and found workout pants and a tank top. Minutes later, I was joining him downstairs as he took out multiple takeout containers. We spread them out on the coffee table and served ourselves dinner. I looked around as I had my first few bites. It had appeared as thought Cooper had been busy for a few hours before I showed up. Almost everything in the living room had been boxed up and from my view of the kitchen, that was nearly done as well.

"How did you know?" I asked him, pointing at the boxes with my fork as I chewed.

"When I didn't hear from you, I called your brother and he filled me in," he replied, refilling his plate with spare ribs. "I figured I could kill two birds with one stone; spend time with you, and help you bring everything home."

I couldn't stop myself from reaching out to touch his cheek. He turned his head and kissed my palm before pulling away to take a bite of his supper. That's when I noticed something was off. He was sitting beside me, but he felt distant all of a sudden. It was like a switch had been flipped since we were upstairs. He avoided making eye contact with me while he finished eating, and he barely made small talk. Just as he was about to get up to put everything away, I moved and straddled him, pinning him to the couch.

"What's going on?"

"Nothing," he lied, moving to kiss me and shift me off of him.

"Oh, hell no." I demanded, as I dug my fingers into the back of the furniture and gripped his hips with my knees. "You don't get to tell me you love me when we are in bed, and disconnect yourself here. It doesn't work that way."

"I know, but you're going to be pissed," he mumbled, laying his head back between my hands.

"That's a great way to start," I said, rolling my eyes.

"It's true," he insisted before his tone grew serious. "You know how I told you I would have to go back to Nashville to finish the album?"

"Yeah…"

"We leave on Friday," he let out in a rush. "We will be gone for two months."

My stomach dropped and the supper I'd just consumed threatened to come right back up. I tried to distance myself and found him locking me against hard muscles as his arms came around me. He buried his face in my neck and kissed the skin left bare by my top. Tears filled my eyes. Unable to contain them, I wrapped my arms around his shoulders and let them slide down my face, untouched.

"Is that why you told me you loved me? Because you hoped that it would lessen the blow for your leaving?"

"I told you I loved you because I do," he snapped, his head

coming back so he could look me in the eye. "You're my everything, Ave. It's only two months. I'm coming back, I promise."

I struggled to believe him. I knew he loved me; he had done everything in his power to show me that. However, all I could picture was myself going to his house when I was eighteen, and finding out that he had left me. The only difference was, this time he was telling me. Maybe that was the key.

"We can talk every day, multiple times a day," he said, bringing one hand up to wipe my tears. "You can come visit once your dad is feeling better."

I froze. My dad would be finishing his treatments this week and Cooper would barely be around for that. How was I going to get through the rest of this without him? I had come to depend on his kisses, his hugs, and his hands to help me forget the bad things. Phone calls and text messages weren't going to be enough. I needed him here.

"I can't do this without you," I told him, tears flowing freely again, harder than before. "You have to stay."

COOPER

"**Y**OU HAVE TO STAY."

Those words in that voice from one of the strongest women I knew, would forever haunt me. As I looked out the airplane window at the clouds below, I could still see her face. The tear tracks running down her cheeks, the pout to her perfect lips, and the total defeat behind it all. I knew I was coming back, yet the fear in the way she looked at me even had me questioning myself. Now I knew why I had left at eighteen without telling her. One word, and I never would have chased my dream. I also realized just how much I had hurt her, how badly I had broken her heart, along with my own.

"It's only two months," Evan reminded me, pulling me out of my own head.

"I know," I sighed. "But you didn't see her face, man."

"I can only imagine," he replied, shaking his head. "You've done right by her this time, Coop. That's got to stand for somethin'."

"I hope so," I agreed. "I told her I loved her, Evan."

"Was that ever in question?" he asked with a grin, eyebrows shooting up his forehead.

"No, I guess not," I chuckled. "Women like to hear it, though."

Evan always knew how to diffuse a serious conversation when it needed to be done. He would definitely help make the next couple of months bearable. The other two, I wasn't so sure about; Chris currently sat on the other side of the plane, two rows up, earbuds in, scribbling on a notepad. Matt was beside him with his eyes closed, dozing lightly.

We had all of first class to ourselves, something I'm sure Chris and Lee had arranged due to the media frenzy as of late. Evan and I had been the first two on and had made ourselves comfortable side by side near the middle, leaving plenty of room for the other two near us so we could all talk on the ride. However, Chris and Matt had boarded after us and, with barely a nod, moved closer to the front, exchanging no words since.

I hadn't thought things had been that tense at the house, but I guess they must have been, since the magazines had come out a week and a half before. Neither of them had gone out of their way to speak to me unless it had to do with the trip. I knew Matt wasn't really upset with me; he just tended to side with Chris, as Evan did with me. Unfortunately, our leader was a hard one to read. He could be pissed because of the negative media attention, adding to his already heavy load of responsibilities, or he could blame me for everything, despite knowing the media outlets were constantly full of shit.

I found it hard to believe that the people I loved the most

were the very ones I was having the hardest time convincing I'd changed. I realized they were the ones I had hurt the worst, yet wasn't family supposed to be about forgiveness? Whether they were blood or not? Weren't they supposed to pick you up when you were down and celebrate alongside you when you achieved your goal?

"Everything will be fine," Evan assured me. "Stop over-thinking."

"I'm turning into a damn woman," I mumbled.

"Nah," my friend commented. "You're just spending too much time between the legs of one."

Knowing he was kidding, but still feeling like I needed to give him hell, I smacked him upside the head. His laugh just got louder, causing me to chuckle along with him. I couldn't wait until he found a woman that brought him to his knees the way Avery had done with me. Payback was a bitch.

It wasn't long before the pilot came on, announcing our descent into Nashville. Lee and our security team would be meeting us at the airport and taking us back to our house. The first couple of days would be crazy while we caught up on stuff and got ready to go back into the studio. I couldn't wait for that. Nothing except for us and our music.

The jolt of the plane touching down brought back the reality that I was no longer in Maine. I felt weird; out of sorts. Funny how easily I had fallen back into the routine of small town life. Not having to look over my shoulder all the time, being able to go out in public without Mikey up my ass, and sleeping with the windows open to listen to the peepers. Lord, it was going to be a long two months.

Evan handed me my carry-on from the overhead compart-ment as we waited for Chris and Matt. Still no words were uttered, but he lifted his head in a "let's go" gesture. We knew the four of us needed to stay close because we weren't sure if anyone had caught wind of our return. Things could get bad real quick, if that happened. Pulling down the sleeves on my long sleeve t-shirt to hide my tattoos and tugging my hat lower on my head, I followed them off the plane. We hadn't even made it halfway down the shoot when we heard the commotion at the gate. Exchanging looks, we all knew we'd already been had.

When the gate came into view, Lee could be seen on his phone, barking at the person on the other end. Mikey and the rest of the security team were holding back a horde of fans and paparazzi. Our manager's hand went up in greeting when he saw us and his face broke into a huge smile. The crowd noise increased a few decibels when they noticed, and all four of us quickly plastered on our public "happy-go-lucky" faces.

"Welcome back, Cooper!" Mikey greeted easily, as he and the others shepherded us past the mob.

"Hey, man," I replied, nodding and smiling to people along the way, and concentrating on keeping a relaxed state to my body.

"You don't look very happy to be here," he observed, carrying on the conversation quietly so others wouldn't hear.

"Is it that noticeable?" I asked, waving to a young boy perched on his father's shoulders, whose hand looked like it was going to fly off from the exuberance of his greeting.

"Only to someone that knows you the way I do," Mikey replied.

I gave a sigh of relief and nudged Matt next to me, to point out a sign a young girl was holding that read "We love Dark Roads!" Things like that never got old. Those people were the reason that we did what we did. They were why we put out the records and played the shows. We weren't doing it for the likes of the media. Matt smiled, gesturing toward the sign, when Chris looked up. Evan, being the goofball he was, ran ahead to the girl and requested her phone. Her eyes were big and full of awe as she handed it to him. He trotted back to us and we wrapped our arms around each other with him in the center, so he could take a selfie. After a couple clicks, he handed her back the phone. Tears filled her eyes and she thanked us more times than I could count as we moved past her.

That moment carried me through the rest of the airport and into the Tahoe that was waiting for us at the curb. I loved what I did, and I just needed to remember times like that. Dark Roads was far from done. We were just at an undeniably large bump, but one that I knew we could get past.

The ride to the house was quiet. When we pulled onto our street, though, a commotion reared its ugly head again. It seemed that, outside our fence, sat thirty or so paparazzi and other members of the media. Seriously? Couldn't they give us a rest? The team handled it with ease, as they always did, and the next thing I knew, we were pulling up to the cabin. It was one of the things that kept Maine with us. It could have easily been picked up, moved to our home state, and looked like it belonged there. Warm and inviting from the outside, once you were in it, you could get lost in the space. It was too much. Sure, we all had plenty of room for ourselves, but it also allowed us to hide from the others. That was not always good for morale.

"Home sweet home," Evan muttered as the vehicle was stopped and turned off.

Evidently, he was just as happy to be here as I was. Grabbing my bag, I slid out behind Matt and walked to the house. Ignoring the rest of the group, I dropped my bag by the door as soon as I was in and made my way to the kitchen. I was starved. We had left Maine just after six this morning and now it was after lunch. Time for food.

I opened the refrigerator and found premade sandwiches waiting. I grabbed the one with my name one it, a bottle of water, and a bag of chips out of a basket on the counter. Matt and Evan followed me in and did the same. We all made ourselves comfortable at the large bar and the silence continued as we ate. Chris had yet to show, so I assumed he and Lee were behind closed doors discussing business.

My phone buzzed in my pocket and I was happy for the distraction. It was a message from Avery, letting me know her father was officially done with treatment and they were stopping at Willie's for a celebratory meal before heading home to rest. I was relieved and could only pray that now Dale would be on the road to recovery. The last week had been especially rough, and I knew both Ave and Keegan were worried about him. I dropped her a response, letting her know we were in Nashville and that I loved her more than she knew. A heart came quickly back from her.

"That Avery?" Matt asked, his mouth full of ham and bread.

"Yeah, Dale is done with his treatments," I told him, grabbing a few more chips.

"Good to hear," he responded.

I nodded my agreement and went back to my food. Now that we were here, I needed to attack my room and figure out what would remain and what needed to be taken back with me. I had already done a good chunk when I left back in April, but now that I knew what the end game was, I could really decide. Finishing my meal, I threw away my trash and grabbed another bottle of water.

"I'm headed up to my room to do some organizing. Let me know if you need me," I informed them as I headed out of the kitchen.

I heard their grunts of response and smiled. Some things never changed.

The house was too quiet. I had never noticed it before.

There was no music, no laughter, no chatter. At my house in Maine, there had been plenty of it. You couldn't get away from it there. Here, you couldn't seem to find it. I was never more sure that I had made the right choice to return home.

Each of us had a suite; we all had a sitting room, our own bathroom, and a bedroom. They were large and could have been their own mini homes. Mine was currently filled with boxes in various packed states, clothes were strewn everywhere. I sighed as I turned on the radio by my couch and got to work.

I didn't realize how long I had been at it until I caught a whiff of barbeque, and my door was flung open. Evan stood in my doorway with two takeout boxes I knew were from my favorite place, The Bull & Boar BBQ. I dropped the box I had been moving and met him at the couch. My mouth watered when I opened the container and took in the sweet smell of the sauce that covered the ribs.

"I didn't even realize I was hungry," I said, eagerly picking up a piece of meat and taking a bite.

"Dude, you would eat Jon's meat, even if you weren't hungry," he chuckled, digging into his own meal.

"True," I answered, laughing.

We had become good friends with the owner, Jon Hampton, after he had noticed our regularity at his corner table. It quickly became the only place where we could eat out without being bothered, and nights when we didn't feel like being in the public eye, he would happily deliver the food himself. It was one of the few things I would miss about being here all the time.

"Heard anything from Chris?" I asked a few moments later.

"Yep, band meeting after breakfast. Eight o'clock," he replied with a grimace.

"Can't even wait for the coffee to kick in, huh?"

"Has he ever?"

I shook my head. We were all early risers, even after a late-night show; but, Chris always had to have our meetings first thing in the morning though, before anyone could even process their coffee enough to function. We suspected it was because this gave him the one-up on us.

The next morning, I had them all beat. I was waiting in our home studio, my my second cup of coffee when they all came in, Lee included. I hadn't been able to sleep without my girl, naked and curled up at my side, so I'd jumped out of bed, hit the gym equipment in the garage, showered, and eaten, before all of them. Chris gave me a surprised look when he found me on the couch with a sketch pad, in the conference room.

"About time you all showed up," I joked as they got settled in.

Evan smirked, the sparkle in his eyes gleaming, while Matt just grumbled. Clearly, he was not in a chipper mood this morning. Chris nodded at me, a small smile playing on his lips, as he sipped from his own cup and took a seat at the end of the table nearest to me. Lee was dressed down, for him, in a button up and jeans – no power suit for us – and his graying hair brushed against the collar of his shirt. He was a trim man and reminded me a lot of the '80s rockers, like Rod Stewart.

"Nice of you to join us today, Cooper," he snapped back with a grin. I was never known for being real good at making these meetings when I was on a binge.

"I figured better late than never." I smiled.

"True," he chuckled. "Now, let's get down to business."

The first half hour was spent going over the new song list, and which ones would be going on the record. The Fourth of July was only a few days away, but the studio was going to remain open, so we could work. It went fairly quickly, as we had already started talking about which songs we wanted when we were back in Maine. Once that was done, everyone got quiet. The next topic of discussion was the future of the band. Our contract was up with the label and we needed to make some decisions where we were headed.

"I'm not sure that we really need to talk about this," Chris finally spoke up. "Cooper and Evan have already made their decisions and unless we replace them, the band doesn't exist anymore."

"What are you talking about?" I asked, my eyes jumping over to Evan, who just shrugged in confusion.

"You two are quitting the band and moving back to Maine," he stated.

"Who said?" Evan asked.

"You two told me you were moving back," Chris replied. "Cooper, you bought a house."

"Yeah, it will be my home base, but I'm not leaving the band," I said. "I just want to settle down a bit."

"Me too," Evan agreed.

"Wait, what?" Chris stammered. "You both told me you were happier in Maine."

"Of course. Wouldn't *you* be, if you had someone like Avery?" I questioned. "I didn't ever say I was done with the band. I want to have my cake and eat it too."

"Exactly!" Evan exclaimed. "There has to be a way we can move north, tour a little, and make records."

Chris and Matt looked back and forth between me and Evan, totally perplexed. Lee leaned against the door, quietly laughing to himself. S0, that was the reason Chris had been such a dick lately; he had assumed Evan and I were done with the band.

"Chris, I'm not that much of an ass that I would leave you hanging without talking to you first," I told him. "Dark Roads was a dream all of us had, not just you."

"Things have just been so damn crazy lately…"

"Yes and no. You just kept thinking that I was going to go

back to the way I was before. You worried about me the most, but had the least faith in my recovery."

You could have heard a pin drop in that room after I said that. He hadn't expected me to say that any more than I had, yet it was true. Chris had stressed about me, not only as his childhood friend, but also as his bandmate. He thought I would fail, like so many before me. He just hadn't taken into consideration that I was me. I was a fighter.

"Holy fuck," Matt muttered beside me.

Chris stood up, body rigid and looking like he was going to beat me to a pulp. I quickly stood because I was not going to take this sitting down. If he was going to strike, I at least wanted a chance. I saw Lee move toward us from where he had been standing.

"You're right," he whispered, moving even closer, so that we were almost nose-to-nose. "I was the one that should have believed in you the most, and I let you down."

"You were protecting yourself and the band when I almost took our dream out," I reminded him, putting my hand on his shoulder. "You didn't let me down. I let myself down."

When he grabbed me in a fierce bear hug, I heard a collective sigh from the other three men in the room. Letting out a deep breathe of my own, I hugged him back just as hard. This was one of my oldest friends and while I hadn't wanted to fight him, I definitely assumed that was where it was headed.

"Enough of that," he joked as he released me. "Let's see if we can come to some type of agreement that we can pitch to the label."

We spent the day working out all the legalities of the changes we wanted to make as a band, and on the business side of things. I couldn't have been happier when we finally finished, and Lee shooed us into the studio for a little playing. He hadn't heard any of the new stuff we had been working on, and was eager for us to show him, so we played, and played, and played. The next thing I knew, it was nine o'clock at night and Maggie and Lexie were bringing us supper.

That night, I slept, soundly, exhaustion from the traveling, sorting out the band stuff, and talking to Avery for a couple of hours, taking over. The next morning, I was just starting to wake when I heard a loud pounding on my door. Before I could get up, Chris opened the door and sticking his head in. I threw a pillow at him and rolled over.

"You have a visitor," he informed me, a little edge to his tone.

"Oh?" I asked, turning to look him.

"Yeah, get your ass dressed and come downstairs."

Well, that didn't sound good. I pulled on my yesterdays jeans and grabbed a questionably-clean t-shirt off the floor before following him. I was just getting the shirt over my head as I made my way down the stairs when I heard a voice that had me cringing.

"Cooper!" Molly screeched.

And that was literally what she did. Her voice sounded like nails on a chalkboard. Why I had ever dated her was beyond me. Her body was rocking and had all the right curves, but her personality and voice left much to be desired. The other three guys stood, leaning against the wall in various states of undress, and Mikey was guarding the door.

"Molly," I greeted, stopping on the next to last step to leave some distance between us. "What can I do for you?"

"We need to talk," she replied in a loud whisper. "Alone."

"How 'bout not," I said. "Either you tell me what you have to say here, in front of the guys, or you, me, and Mikey can go in the living room and you can do it there."

"Oh, Coop, what are you afraid of?" she asked, moving closer to me and reaching out to stroke a finger down my arm.

Mikey quickly moved to pull her back a bit, and the guys all shook their heads. There was no way that I was going to allow myself to be alone with this woman. I didn't need any more bad publicity, and it would just turn into a "he said, she said" story.

"I'm not afraid of anything," I told her, moving up a step, "but I don't appreciate you spinning lies that involve me, in order to better your career."

"Who said they were lies?" she asked innocently.

"You sure as hell aren't pregnant," I pointed out, her pants fitting her like a second skin and her crop top showing off her fit stomach. "Nor are we getting married."

"You know how the media is," she admonished, flicking her wrist like she was dismissing it all. "As for us, well, that isn't over yet."

"Oh yes, it is," I heard Maggie speak up from the hallway. "I believe he told you that a while ago. If you keep insisting, we can file a restraining order or a lawsuit against you. Which would you prefer?"

I coughed and had to cover my mouth in order to hide the smirk and the laugh that was threatening. I saw the guys all do the same. Molly's face turned five shades of red as she stomped her foot and clenched her fists, sending her bracelets jangling. I could see her trying to put together a comeback, but when Maggie was in lawyer mode, she was a tough one to go up against.

"We could help each other's careers, ya know," Molly sputtered, as she spun on her heel and tried to open the door.

"Let me help you with that," Mikey offered, opening it with ease.

Once she could leave, she took a deep breath and plastered a smile on her face before stepping out on the porch. It was all for show. We had pissed her off, but she wasn't going to let the paparazzi see her down and out. It wouldn't help her cause.

"Wow," Evan sighed. "Can that woman put on a show, or what? I swear she is like Dr. Jekyll and Mr. Hyde."

"Ain't that the truth!" I agreed, coming the rest of the way down the stairs.

"Time for breakfast," Matt announced as we all turned to head to the kitchen, only to find Lexie standing in the doorway, looking down at her phone.

"What's going on, darlin'?" I asked, stepping around Chris.

"You need to go home. It's Dale."

AVERY

TODAY WAS THE DAY; THE final treatment for my father. It was a blessing and a curse, all at the same time. His battle wasn't over, but it would be nice not to have to go to the hospital every day. Hopefully he would start feeling better too. It had been a roller coaster ride the past six weeks. Some days were good, and some were bad. This week had been the toughest yet.

Sighing, I rolled over and pulled the extra pillow on my bed to my face. When I inhaled slightly, I could still smell Cooper's shampoo and cologne clinging to the fabric. It pulled at my heart, but comforted me as well. I knew he didn't want to be gone, but it didn't make his absence any easier. The early morning kiss he gave me before he left for Nashville still lingered on my lips. Knowing I couldn't physically touch him soon caused my eyes to sting.

Before I could lose myself in self-pity, I reached over to turn off the alarm, and climbed out of bed. It had been a long night last night, with Dad up every couple of hours between the muscle pain and the dry heaves. I yawned and padded my way to the hallway. Poking my head into my father's room, I found him sleeping comfortably. Feeling slightly better, I made my way to the bathroom and took the hottest shower I could stand. My muscles instantly loosened with the temperature of the water, and it helped to wake me up a bit.

Knowing it was going to be a muggy day, I slid into jean shorts and a tank top, making sure to grab a button up for the hospital to ward off the chill of the air conditioner. I was just putting my sandals on when I heard the front door open and close, followed by soft voices. Confused, I made my way to the kitchen.

"Hey," I greeted my brother and sister-in-law, surprised. "I thought we were meeting for lunch after dad's radiation?"

"We were," Keegan answered, wrapping an arm around my shoulders and kissing my temple, "but we wanted to be here for you and Dad. I can't tell you how much it has meant to me that you have shouldered a lot of this on your own."

"What are you talking about?" I asked, wrapping my arm around his back and reaching out to take Abby's hand in mine. "You've been taking care of the business and your wife."

"I know," he responded, his voice soft. "I still feel like I should have done more."

I squeezed him and waved them both off. As far as I was concerned, my brother had done plenty. Grind was the most important thing to my father, other than us kids. It was crucial that the business continued to thrive, and he had done a wonderful job at that.

"You guys sit, and I'll make breakfast," I told them, moving to the refrigerator to grab the eggs.

Never being one to listen or sit still in the kitchen, Abby got up and proceeded to help me. I heard movement from the master bedroom while we were cooking, and Keegan quickly got up to make sure that Dad was all set. Just as we were setting mugs of coffee, tea, and hot chocolate on the table, the two of them came out. My brother plastered a smile on his face, but I could see the weariness behind it. My father looked tired and pale, but dismissed us all when we tried to help him.

Knowing a fight would be futile, I went back to the counter to grab the plates of bacon and scrambled eggs. We kept the meal light and stuck to things we thought my father would be able to eat. Once I put them down on the table, I grabbed a yogurt from the refrigerator for good measure. I had a feeling he wouldn't eat much, but anything was worth a shot.

Breakfast was a quiet affair, everyone lost in their own thoughts; mostly my brother and I fretting over my father eating something substantial. When all was said and done, I think he had taken a total of three bites of egg and had finished his tea and his yogurt. I was happy with the small victory.

Abby and I shooed the guys off while we cleaned. My father shuffled off to the bathroom to get ready for the day, with Keegan hovering in the hallway to make sure he was all set. Now I knew why I had left him to the business; he would have driven my father crazy the entire time. I fretted inside and kept the cool exterior I knew my dad needed. He was still a man, after all. He didn't want to depend on anyone.

"He's going to drive you nuts in the delivery room," I informed Abby, as I gestured at my brother.

"How about now?" she chuckled. "If I let out just the slightest peep, he is on me like flies to poop. He is so attentive, it's both annoying and sweet."

"He was like that when I was growing up," I reminisced, drying my hands on a towel. "You should have seen him on Thanksgiving, when Rick tackled me a little too hard while we were playing football. Poor kid hid in the kitchen with the adults the rest of the day so that Keeg couldn't get to him."

"Oh my," she giggled and sighed. "He's going to be such a good father."

"The best," I assured her, squeezing her arm as I made my way by her.

Once my father was ready for the day, almost an hour later, we all piled into my car. Despite our protesting and the fact that he felt awful, my father insisted we still stop at the job site. Keegan finally gave in and said it would be a good excuse to check on Rick's progress without him. Abby and I weren't thrilled with the idea, but again, I wouldn't take what little independence he had from him. I just couldn't do it.

Pulling into the site, I saw Dad instantly relax. This was his passion. This was where everything else disappeared. Working and being around the guys was what fueled him. These visits, probably more than us, was what was getting him through the bad days. Here, he wasn't treated like a patient, like a sick father, like a man with cancer. Here, he was just the man who ran the company.

"You've got a half-hour at most, old man; otherwise, we'll be late," Keegan told him as we all climbed from the car.

I giggled at the look on Dad's face as he waved off Keegan's comment. The two of them walked toward the building while Abby and I hung back. We were in the next town over and the structure was going to be two stories. From my understanding, it was going to house four separate businesses' offices. Maybe i should talk to Keegan to see if any were available for Lane.

"Have you talked to Jen at all?" Abby asked, breaking into my thoughts after a few moments.

"Nope," I replied. "Not since I sent her the text message letting her know I didn't need her dropping off every magazine that trash talked Coop."

"She's just worried about you, ya know," my sister-in-law defended.

"I get that," I told her. "But do you see Dad and Keegan being that harsh? They have more reason to want him out of the picture than she does."

"True," she mused. "Cooper does seem like a decent guy."

"He is," I sighed. "He messed up when we were kids, but we were just that; kids. I know why he did what he did. Does it still hurt? Hell yes, however, he is trying really hard to make it right."

"Those magazines can't make it easy though," she said.

"They don't," I agreed. "But his arms around me and his support through all of this makes it much easier to stomach them."

"Just don't give up on her," she remarked. "You two have been friends a long time too."

"I won't," I replied. "She just needs to support my decisions."

Abby nodded and looped her arm through mine. We stood there, watching my father, Keegan, and Rick converse, and all seemed okay with the world. A little color was seeping back into my dad's cheeks and even the stress from earlier seemed to have melted away from Keegan. Maybe we would actually be able to celebrate the end of his treatments, at least a little bit.

Eventually, it was time to wrangle the men back into the car and head to the hospital. The last round of radiation was fairly uneventful, the only surprise coming when my father teared up at not seeing the nurses any more. He had become fairly attached to a couple of them, and I'm pretty sure I saw one of the older ladies slip him her number when we were on our way out the door. They had been amazing to him and for that, I would be eternally grateful. Going every day had been tolerable, thanks to them.

"Stop in at Willie's," I told my brother as we started the drive back home.

He gave me a funny look, but did as I told him when we got there. I had texted Will ahead of time and asked if he could put together a little something for my dad. I knew Dad wouldn't be up to the normal bar food, but my friend let me know he would take care of it. I was surprised when we pulled in and the parking lot had quite a few cars. He normally was pretty quiet around lunch time on a weekday.

"What's going on here?" my father asked as we pulled to a stop.

"I have no clue," I told him honestly. "I thought we would stop in a grab a bite to eat before we headed home."

He smiled and nodded in appreciation. When we were on our way to the door, he put his arm around my shoulders and pulled me close to kiss me on the cheek. The display of affection made my eyes fill, and I put my arm around his thin waist and gave him a squeeze. Dale Cyr was not one for PDA, so I was going to bask in what I could get.

Opening the door, Keegan ushered us in ahead of him. My dad froze, bringing me to a stop since he still had ahold of me. The place was filled with the Hall family, Cooper excluded, and his employees. I found Willie with my eyes, standing near the bar, and he smiled at me. I nodded and rolled my eyes to the ceiling to keep from bawling like a baby. My father seemed just as moved as I was, blinking his eyes repeatedly to keep the tears at bay. I kissed him on the cheek and stepped back to allow others to see him.

"He looks good, even with everything he has been through," I heard a familiar voice say from beside me.

Turning, I found Jen. We hadn't spoken much since that morning at the shop and I hadn't seen her face-to-face at all. Her long hair was pulled back in a ponytail and her face was filled with sadness. I had always hated fighting with her, but her strong will had always gotten the best of our relationship. She took my hand in hers and looked down at them as our fingers intertwined.

"I'm sorry," she whispered, "for everything."

I couldn't respond or hold back the tears any longer. I pulled her into my arms and hugged her with all I was worth. Jen didn't hesitate and held me just as tightly. It had bothered me more than I had let on that morning, when she stormed in on Cooper and myself. He encouraged me to talk to her since then, I flat out refused. Hopefully, she would learn to accept him in my life.

"Come on, ladies, no more blubbering," Will admonished. "We are supposed to be celebrating."

I let go of my friend and hastily wiped at my eyes and face, only to find my hands replaced with much larger ones. He took to gently drying my tears, with a soft napkin from his apron before he pulled me into his arms. I took comfort in his warmth and gave him a hard squeeze of thanks for all he had done. When Willie pulled back and seemed satisfied that I looked okay, he led us over to the buffet table.

We spent the next couple of hours socializing and listening to stories about my dad in his youth and tales from the work-sites. Keegan and I contributed every once in a while, but for the most part, we just took it all in. My father was more animated than I had seen him since he had started his treatments. I'm not sure how many times I thanked my friends for their part in it, yet they both waved it off. They loved having my dad around, and being able to repay him for some of what he had done for them growing up was a bonus.

"I think it's time to head home," Keegan said a little while later, pointing to my father.

For the first time since we had arrived, he was sitting in a chair by himself, watching people. His color had paled again, and I could see the struggle he was having at keeping his eyes open. I nodded, and he headed toward him while I went to the bar to let Willie know we were leaving.

"Hey, Will," I greeted when I reached him. "We're going to head for home. Dad is worn out."

"Not a problem," he assured me. "I'll pack up this stuff and bring some of it by later. That way, you won't have to cook."

"You're the best," I told him. "Thanks again for everything."

"It's nothing, really," he replied. "We're practically family. I'll see you later."

I waved to him and turned to follow my family out the door. Jen caught me before I could go, and the two of us agreed to breakfast the following morning. Things finally seemed to be going in the right direction with her. I headed outside behind my sister-in-law, and noticed that my father seemed to be fading fast; Keegan was all but holding him up on the way to the car. I ran ahead and opened the passenger door for them.

We had barely pulled out of the parking lot when his breathing shallowed and he started dozing. I met Keegan's worried eyes in the rearview mirror and threw him a reassuring smile. It wasn't uncommon for him to tire easily after a treatment, though I was concerned he may have overdone it with all the visiting. Pulling into the driveway, I leaned over and shook him gently to wake him.

He was disoriented at first, looking at my brother in a panic, but realizing we were home seemed to calm him. That was something new, but I guess I had done it a time or two when I was woken up unexpectedly and unsure of where I was. We all helped him in and while Keegan and Abby got him settled in his bedroom, I grabbed a bottle of water for him from the refrigerator.

It wasn't long before he was out once again, and the three of us went back to the living room. My body wasn't far behind my father's. The minute I sat down, I felt the prior night catch up with me. Abby made sure the Hallmark Channel was quietly playing on the television, while I felt my brother lay a light blanket over me. The kiss he brushed across my temple was the last thing I remembered before dozing off.

"DOES SHE ALWAYS SLEEP THIS soundly?" I heard Rick ask none too quietly.

"That's a question for Cooper," Willie answered stiffly, "not me."

I didn't want to know why Will's answer was so brusque, but I quickly remembered the black eyes that Coop had attributed to his brother. Did Will have feelings for me? He had never said anything. Oh geez, so not what I needed right now. One Hall brother was enough.

"Maybe I should sit on her," Rick suggested.

That comment had my eyes flying open, only to find the youngest Hall brother grinning at me from across the living room. I threw a pillow at him, causing him to chuckle, and stretched before getting up. Will was in the kitchen, putting containers in the refrigerator.

"Sorry, Ave," he apologized as he put the last one in. "I wouldn't have brought him if I had known you were sleeping."

"It's okay," I replied, throwing Rick a mock glare. "I needed to get up, otherwise I wouldn't sleep tonight."

"We're not staying anyway," Willie told me as he moved past me to the living room. "Come on, Rick."

"You guys can stay for supper if you want," I told them, fighting back a yawn.

"It looks like you need more sleep," Will chuckled in return. "Eat something and get back to bed."

"Good night, sweetheart," Rick called as he followed his brother out the door.

I waved to them both before it shut with a soft *click* and did just as he instructed. I finished, and wondered if my father was still sleeping. I hadn't heard a noise from his bedroom and was starting to get a little nervous. Figuring he might be hungry, I warmed up some broth and put it in a travel mug for him, before grabbing crackers and another of bottle of water. Keegan had left the bedroom door ajar, so I nudged it with my hip and found that he was sitting up and looking around.

The look on his face was just like the one that he'd had in the car when he woke up. He seemed a little disoriented and unsure, yet his face calmed and lit up when he saw me. His eyes were dull, and his color was pasty, but he moved on his own, so I took that as a good sign.

"How are you doing?" I asked as I handed him his mug.

He shrugged as he took a sip. The bottle from earlier hadn't been touched. I looked from him to the water and back, only to receive another shrug. Men were worse than children sometimes!

"Don't you remember the conversation about getting dehydrated?"

"Yeah, yeah," he mumbled, taking another sip of broth and putting the cup on the side table. "I'm an adult, ya know."

I laughed slightly at his attitude – the fight sure hadn't left him – and helped him to get comfortable again on his side. His eyes dropped quickly once he moved, and his breathing turned shallow. I checked his forehead quickly for any sign of warmth and there didn't seem to be any. Satisfied that he had probably just overdone it that afternoon, I took the warm water bottle back to the kitchen with me.

It was still early, but, my body was wiped. Even though I would probably end up waking up way too early, I decided that bed was the best place to be. I was sure that Cooper would wake me up at some point, with a phone call, once he could get away. He and the guys had been meeting all day to work things out with the band and what they were going to do about their label. I hoped they could all come to an agreement.

No sooner did my head hit the pillow, I was out. A vague recollection of talking to my man for a couple of hours filtered in as I struggled to wake up the following morning. I groaned when I looked at the clock, and saw that it was much later than my normal wake-up time. Obviously, my body had needed the catch up. Not bothering to shower, since I was late getting up and Jen would be here any time, I pulled on clean clothes and washed up before going in to check on my father.

That's when I noticed it. The house seemed abnormally quiet. Not that it was ever loud with just the two of us, but there were no outside noises. Even the hum from the refrigerator in the kitchen wasn't there. A chill went through my body and I rushed into my father's room. He hadn't moved from the night before and was still on his side. When I went to him, I noticed that his face had turned an ashen color and his breathing was so shallow, I almost couldn't tell if he was. Moving the blankets back, I searched for a pulse; it was slow and faint, but it was there.

Shaking him lightly at first and calling to him didn't stir him. Trying again a little harder, and with more force, I raised my voice and got nothing. I took a deep breath and reached for his cell phone to call 9-1-1. I heard the front door open and close while I kept trying to wake my father, holding the phone to my ear.

"Avery?"

"In here, Jen," I called, my voice steadier than I felt.

"9-1-1, what is your emergency?"

"I need an ambulance at 45 Mill Creek Road as soon as possible," I told the operator. "My father is unresponsive."

"What's going on?" I heard my friend ask, at the same time that the woman in my ear was trying to get more information.

"I can't wake him up," I told her quickly. "Can you please go get my cell phone and call my brother?"

While she was gone, I rattled off information to the operator and sat down on the bed, still rubbing my father's back, hoping for some kind of reaction. Jen returned, phone to her ear, and I could hear my brother on the other end. While the 9-1-1 woman dispatched the ambulance, I swapped phones long enough to fill him and tell him to meet us at the hospital. Just as I was taking back my father's phone, I could hear the sirens. Jen ran to the door to let them in, and I felt the weight of everything resting on my shoulders.

The paramedics came in and I hung up. They drilled me with questions about my father's medical history and I answered them rapid fire. The assessment was short before they went back out to get the gurney. I heard Jen on the phone and just barely registered when she growled in frustration.

"That damn man," I heard her mutter.

Looking at her, she waved at me to ignore her and I saw her continue to scroll through my contacts. She finally seemed to find who she was looking for and hit *Send* before putting the phone to her ear, while grabbing my hand with her free one. We walked out behind the paramedics, my stomach turning as they continued to talk in what seemed like code as they went. An IV was started and his shirt was cut open, so they could attach patches to monitor his heart. I felt like I was going to collapse, just as I heard Jen say into the phone...

"Tell Cooper to come home now. Something is wrong with Dale, and Avery needs him."

COOPER

ALTHOUGH I HAD TRAVELED ALL over the world for ten years, never had one trip taken so long. The moment Lexie had uttered the words "Avery needs you," I had been moving. I stumbled my way back to my bedroom, with Evan hot on my heels to keep me from falling on my face, and blindly packed a carry-on. Seconds later, I was slipping on my cowboy boots, not even caring that I hadn't showered and was wearing dirty clothes, and was racing back down the stairs. Mikey was at the door, waiting to drive me to the airport, and the other three were right behind me, with bags in tow.

"You guys don't need to…" I stammered, trying to find words to tell them that they didn't need to come with me, but that it meant the world to me that they wanted to.

"You and Avery need us," Chris said, cutting me off. "We're coming. The record can wait a couple more weeks."

I nodded and did my best to hold back the tears threatening to spill. My girl needed me. *Got to get it together, Hall*, I told myself, as Mikey opened the door and started to usher us out.

"Everything will be all set by the time you get to the airport," Maggie assured us, as she held the phone to her ear and kissed us quickly on the cheeks before we got in the Tahoe.

Sitting in the backseat between Matt and Evan, my right leg bounced anxiously. I wanted to snap my fingers and be there, holding Avery in my arms, assuring her everything would be okay. I hated that I didn't know what was going on, other than that she needed me, and Dale wasn't doing well. Those pieces of information alone were digging a hole in my stomach, never mind what it was doing to my heart.

"We'll get there, man," Evan said, putting his hand on my knee to stop the jiggling. "Everything will be okay."

I wanted to hit something, namely him right now, and ask him how he knew that it would be. How did he know that Dale wouldn't die before we got back? How did he know that Avery wouldn't hate me for leaving her again, and not being there when she needed me the most? The look on his face was the only thing that kept me from flipping out. His eyes were their normal bright blue and calm, while his smile was reassuring and never faltered.

Sighing, I stilled my leg and laid my head against the back of the seat, looking at the ceiling. We were just pulling into the airport when I put my hand to my pocket and realized that I didn't have my cell phone. Starting to panic, I grabbed my bag and dug through it. Still not finding it, and about to tell Mikey to turn around, I caught Chris looking at me from the front seat. He held my phone in his hand, and I watched as he dropped it into his bag and zipped it.

"What the hell, man?" I growled, leaning toward him. "Give it back. I need to text Avery."

"No way," he told me. "She needs to concentrate on her father. Will is keeping us posted on what is going on."

I saw red and only because Matt and Evan were now holding my arms, did I not lunge at Chris. I needed to hear her voice. I needed to know that she was okay, and let her know I was coming as fast as I fucking could. I struggled against their hold, but neither of them would give.

"How could you do that to me?" I asked, my voice strangled with emotion.

"You will go crazy if we don't," Chris said, his voice just as strained as mine.

I shook the guys off and leaned back again. They were right. It *would* drive me crazy if I messaged her and she didn't respond. She also needed to worry about her father and not her boyfriend. I just ached to be there to support her. I also knew how much the guys loved Avery and her family, so this had to be almost as hard on them as it was for me. I started to apologize, but Chris just waved me off and checked the incoming text message on his phone. It must have been our flight itinerary because he directed Mikey to a little road off the main cluster.

Those of us in the back looked at each other in confusion. We were no longer headed to the main airport, but toward a hangar off to the side that looked like it housed private planes. What the hell?

"Maggie has a client that has his own private jet," Chris informed us as Mikey pulled to a stop. "Looks like she called in a favor to get us home."

We would owe that guy lifetime tickets to our concerts, but none of us cared at that point. Jumping out of the SUV behind Evan, we all jogged to the plane waiting for us. The direct flight would get us there so much more quickly than the commercial would have, and for that, I was grateful. Once we were settled into the plane and starting to taxi down the runway, I was starting to feel a little better. *I'm on my way, baby*, I whispered, wishing I could talk to her.

My leg started to bounce again as soon as we were in the air. I knew that the flight would go quickly, but we still had an hour drive home once we landed. It just wasn't fast enough. Time travel really needed to be invented so that people could get where they needed to before they missed important things. I wasn't one to pray, however that day, as we made our way back to Maine, I did. I hoped for Dale's recovery, I wished for Avery's forgiveness, and I longed for my crazy as fuck life to calm down.

Hours later, we were touching down. I started getting more antsy and Evan put his hand on my shoulder to calm me. I shrugged him off and looked out the window. It felt good to know I was back in the same state as her, yet it still wasn't close enough. I saw that we were heading toward a hangar that sat off from the rest of the airport, just like it had been in Nashville, and next to it was a black Tahoe. It was like *déjà vu*. I followed Chris off the plane and all four of us jogged to the vehicle.

A man about the size of Mikey was waiting at the vehicle with all the doors open and he gave us a subtle nod when we climbed in. Chris again took shotgun and proceeded to fill the driver in on where we needed to go as soon as we were all buckled in. They spoke quietly as we pulled out into the winding roads that surrounded the airport and we headed for the highway.

The ride might have only been an hour, but damn, did it feel so much longer. The landscape passed in a blur, and I knew I was bouncing my leg again without meaning to. Chris had heard very little from my brother in terms of Dale's condition. Basically, they were running tests and he had been unresponsive when Avery found him that morning. I could only imagine what my girl was going through. I'm glad, though, that my family, and hers, were there for her when I couldn't be.

"Could you drive a little faster?" I murmured, wiping my hands down my face.

"Almost there, brother," Evan muttered. "Almost there."

I could see that the others were starting to get anxious as well. Chris kept checking his phone, Matt was drumming out a beat on his leg with his fingers, and Evan was tapping on the SUV door. I'm sure none of them realized it any more than I did, with my leg hopping like a jumping bean. It made me feel a little better, knowing they were just as worried and ready to get there as I was.

The exit we needed was up next, and I straightened in my seat. Fifteen more minutes I thought, just fifteen more minutes. Chris's phone *dinged*, signaling a text message and I zeroed my attention in on him. He shook his head and his fingers flew across the screen, responding to the text.

"Rick is going to meet us down by the emergency room doors. They have him there. Everyone is waiting in a private waiting room, since there are so many of them, and we're coming," he told us once he was done.

I nodded. I felt bad that they had to do this due to our fame, but I had to be there. Avery needed me; she told me so before I left. When our driver pulled into the hospital parking lot, I was ready to climb over Evan to get out. My friend stuck his arm out, so I wouldn't plow him over, and opened the door as soon as the vehicle came to a stop. I jumped out behind him, not bothering to wait for the others. I couldn't.

Rick was at the sliding glass doors when they opened and turned, motioning for us to follow. I caught up to him, almost on his heels, as we rounded a corner, and he held up a hand to stop us. When I entered the room, everyone stood up. Keegan and Abby were closest to the door and I could see the relief in their eyes when they saw that we had arrived. My parents were there, along with Willie and, much to my surprise, Jen and her husband.

"Where is she?" I asked them, not caring who answered.

"She's in with him now. They are only allowing one visitor at a time," Keegan said as he approached me. "I'm so glad you're here."

I hugged him tightly. I couldn't stand seeing the worry in his eyes. He was such a strong man, just like his father, and it killed me to see him so broken. I couldn't understand how the world could do this to people like them. He should have been beside himself with happiness that his wife was carrying their first child; instead, he was stressing about keeping his father's business afloat and whether or not he would lose him.

"I need to see her," I told him as I released him and moved to the door.

"You can't, Cooper," my dad said, stepping in front of me. "You need to wait until she comes back."

"I'm not waiting," I replied, moving to go around him.

Nothing was going to keep me from seeing her now. Not even a few nurses or doctors. The activity in this part of the hospital was a constant buzz. A few people glanced at me as I approached the nurse's station. I saw the moment that recognition settled in with a couple of the staff. Before I got a chance to ask where the Cyrs were, I heard the voice that belonged to the person I was looking for.

"Cooper?" I turned, and there she stood. "What are you doing here?"

"Jen called Lexie," I told her, closing the distance between us I reached for her when I was close enough.

"You didn't need to come," she told me as I embraced her. "We're fine, and you have an album to finish."

She didn't put her arms around me, and I felt her stiffen up when I pulled her against my chest. Putting her back at arm's length, I looked at her. She was clearly upset, yet emoted strength. Her eyes were hard.

"You're more important than some fucking album," I growled, keeping my voice low.

"I'm sure," she spat out. "That's why you left again when I needed you."

There it was. Everything we had worked to get past came slamming into me. She had told me she understood and that she loved me too. Now, thanks to whatever the hell was going on with her father, we were back to being eighteen years old again. I stepped to the side, bringing her with me so that we were against the wall outside of her father's room.

"You know better," I told her. "I love you more than anything. You are the air that I breathe. If I could have snapped my fingers and been here when it happened, I would have been."

I felt her soften a bit under my hands, but I could sense she wasn't completely convinced. I pulled her into my arms again and this time, hers came around me. She didn't snuggle in like she usually did; but, she sank into me a little bit more. I nuzzled into her neck and kissed the sensitive spot behind her ear.

"I should have been here. You're going to have to be patient with me while we work through this," I apologized.

"You're still an asshole," she said against my chest as she latched onto me.

"Yeah, well, that's a given," I told her with a chuckle. "How's your dad?"

"Dehydrated, and his sugar levels are all kinds of screwy," she replied, pulling away enough to wipe at the tears that had escaped. "Coop, I couldn't wake him up."

Her tears started flowing harder. I gathered her up against me and tangled one of my hands in her hair, anchoring her to me. Her hands dug at my back as though she wanted to climb into my skin to escape her own. She fought back the sobs that strained to come out. I rubbed my free hand up and down her back, whispering soothing words to her. She was breaking my heart.

Finally, she started to calm down. Her breathing steadied and her quiet cries turned to hiccups. My shirt was soaked from where her face was pressed against me, but I didn't care. I leaned back enough so that I could wipe her cheeks with my thumbs, and planted a soft kiss on her forehead. She sighed.

"I was just heading to get Keegan, so he could come sit with him for a bit," she told me when she could speak.

"No problem," I replied, turning back to the waiting room. "I couldn't wait until you came back to see you."

Her smile was quick. She leaned into me as I put my arm around her shoulder, and she wrapped one of her arms around me in return. We hadn't made it two steps when all hell seemed to break loose. The steady beeping of the monitor in Dale's room started going off in one steady beep, along with a bunch of other machines shrieking and wailing. Avery pivoted, and I had to shift quickly to grab her around the waist to keep her from going back in behind the nurses and doctors running to his bedside.

"Cooper!" she screeched. "Let me go!"

"Let them work, Ave," I whispered, holding her tightly as she thrashed, footsteps coming up behind me.

"Paddles!" someone hollered. "Clear!"

"Daddy!"

AVERY

9 months later

THE HOUSE WAS QUIET AS I padded to the kitchen. Sunlight was just starting to peek through the trees, and I should have been sleeping like the others, but I was too anxious. After making a cup of hot chocolate, I took my mug out to the back deck to watch the rest of the sunrise.

It was supposed to be a gorgeous spring day, according to the weatherman and, for once, it seemed he would actually be right. There wasn't a cloud to be seen. I shivered a bit with the early morning chill. Taking a quick sip of the warm liquid remedied that and I warmed from the inside out. Squirrels chattered as they woke in the trees, and I chuckled as two of them chased

194 | MARCIE SHUMWAY

each other from one branch to the next. It was the perfect start to a perfect day.

Closing my eyes, I inhaled through my nose and exhaled through my mouth a couple of times. My nerves slowly started to relax, yet my stomach continued to jump. How did people do this more than once in their life? Once was enough for me.

"I figured I'd find you out here," Julie commented, coming out the sliding glass doors with a mug of coffee in her hand.

"I couldn't sleep," I confessed, snuggling down deeper into my sweatshirt.

"No doubt," she replied, sitting down beside me. "I was the same way."

"Me too," Jen agreed, coming out with Abby in tow.

"Me three," was the concensus from my sister-in-law.

"Why?" I questioned, sitting up. "You know you want to spend the rest of your life with this person, and you love them so much the idea of being without them hurts. Why would you be nervous about marrying them?"

"I think it's just the idea of that deeper, life-long commitment," Julie theorized. "Regardless of how much you love the person, it can be pretty scary."

"I totally agree," Abby nodded. "Coupled with the idea of having all eyes on you."

"Exactly!" I exclaimed. "He's used to that, I'm not. If it weren't for his parents, I would have eloped."

They all chuckled. Who was I kidding? I had loved every step of the process, from picking the flowers to finding that flawless dress. The girls had been amazing, helping with everything and anything along the way. It had truly been a breeze, and was far from the horror stories I'd heard.

"Chop, chop, ladies," came an order from the doors. "It's time to eat breakfast, so we can get this show on the road."

Oh, did I mention Lexie being my maid of honor might have been the best decision I had ever made? I struggled with choosing between the other girls, so rather than hurt any of their feelings, I asked Lex. She was a perfect fit from the get-go, and the major reason it had all flowed so well.

"I should probably call my mom anyway, and check on Emma," Abby said, getting up first.

I smiled at her back as she went into the house. This had been her first night away from the baby and, despite a crying session early on the previous evening, she had handled it rather well. My brother, on the other hand, called his mother-in-law so many times that she had finally called us. Only after an hour-long conversation reminding him that Connie raised Abby by herself, had he calmed down. I was pretty sure the guys handing him drinks helped too.

"Are you okay?" I asked Julie, as Jen went into the house with Lexie, while she had yet to move.

"Yeah," she sighed. "Just thinking."

"Anything you want to talk about?"

"Umm…today is your day, darling," she reminded me. "My problems can wait for another day."

Knowing she would stay true to her word, I grabbed her hand and pulled her up, absently noticing she didn't have her wedding band on. Once she was standing, I tucked her hand in the crook of my arm and led her to the door. Letting her go ahead of me, I turned and looked at the backyard of my childhood home. This would be the last time I would enjoy a sunrise here. After today, I would no longer live here, and I couldn't decide if that made me happy or sad.

Breakfast flew by and before I knew it, the hairdressers showed up. Lexie had hooked us up with a couple of stylists she knew from Nashville. They were good at their jobs and worked efficiently. The ladies kept us distracted with stories from the entertainment world, which helped the time pass quickly.

"You relax for a bit," Jen said, once she and the other bridesmaids were all done up. "We'll go put our dresses on and show you the entire package."

I laughed as they raced for the bedrooms like little girls, giggling as they went. They all warmed my heart. As different as they all were, we all melded together. We held each other up and had become as close as sisters. It was a bond I would forever be grateful for, and never thought I could have since i only had a brother.

"What do you think?" Julie asked, coming out first.

"Oh my!" I gasped. "You look amazing!"

The dresses were royal blue, knee length numbers with halter tops. Coop and I had given each of them a necklace, with a small guitar pick as the charm, and I'd had their names with our wedding day engraved on the back. It was the only jewelry they wore. Brown cowboy boots stitched with the same vibrant color as the dresses completed the ensemble. My boots would match theirs.

"We have to keep up with you," Julie joked with a wink.

I snapped pictures of the girls in various poses, setting us off in another fit of giggles. One request I had for the day was only to have the photographer at the ceremony and reception. I wanted the girls and I to have our alone time. There would be enough paparazzi and crap when we got there.

"Come on lady, your turn," Lexie said, taking my hand and leading me toward my bedroom.

I stopped when I entered the room and took in the sight of my dress hanging from the closet door with the train flowing onto the floor. I had opted for a strapless gown even though I wasn't normally a dress person. The fabric molded to my form, and the slight dip in the front of the sweetheart neckline would give my new husband a glimpse of the cleavage he always appreciated. Tiny sequins covered the entire bodice while the skirt was smooth. I had opted for a princess silhouette, so I would still get a little flare, but I didn't want to look like the princesses in the movies. I wanted to be comfortable.

"Everything okay?" Jen asked, coming up behind me.

"Yeah," I told her, content for the first time that day. "It's just perfect."

Her face broke into a knowing smile. I took the dress down and shooed her from the room. I could zip it up for the most part on my own, and I wanted to give them the whole picture at once. I slid off my comfy clothes, leaving me clad in only a wisp of white lacy underwear. I wanted as little between my skin and the dress as possible. I had a feeling it would be off the minute the wedding was over anyway. Gingerly, I stepped the gown and slid it up my body.

Once I had it on, I zipped what I could and took a deep breath. The mirror was at my back and I slowly turned around so that I could see myself. I was stunned. My hair was done in waves, with only a little pulled up on the top to keep it out of my face. It was pinned back with a few pieces of baby's breath. I wore the same necklace as the girls, but I had diamond hoops adorning my ears; they were a gift from Keegan. The diamond on my finger sparkled against the sequins where my hand rested.

"Holy hell," I murmured with a smile.

I put my boots on and opened the door. I could hear the girls chatting in the living room. As I got closer, their voices quieted. Stepping around the corner into the room, I presented myself to them. They were silent. If I hadn't seen the tears or the hands over their mouths, I would have been insulted by the lack of comments. They were literally speechless.

"He is going to be blown away," Lexie finally whispered, when she could find her voice.

"Perfect," I replied, my own voice shaking.

Tears were wiped away, makeup was retouched, and extra hairspray was applied. Just as we were finishing up, the limo pulled into the driveway. Hiking up my dress, we made our way outside, with Jen and Julie helping to make sure that my train didn't touch the ground. I was so engrossed in what we were doing that I didn't notice who had come with the car until a long low whistle was heard.

"Damn, woman!" Mikey exclaimed. "You're going to put that man on his ass."

"That's the idea," I laughed, throwing him a wink and feeling my cheeks warm.

We piled into the car for the brief drive, but we were held up when we turned up the long drive. I realized now why Mikey was there, people were everywhere! So much for our careful plan to keep the guest list to two hundred people; the paparazzi and fans had arrived in droves. I closed my eyes and took some deep breaths. Everyone around me would make sure this went off without a hitch; I just needed to have faith in them. Opening my eyes again, I found Lexie busy texting and whispering with Julie. They had it under control.

The limo was finally able to pull up to the front of the house. Mikey came around and opened the door for us, the girls getting out first to ensure that I wasn't seen by the photographers before the groom saw me. The all-clear was given, and we all but dashed from the car to the front door. The guests were already out back, so we congregated in the living room of the old farmhouse, the house that now belonged to me and my fiance. Our new beginning, as husband and wife.

The back door stood open and on Lexie's signal, everyone settled into their seats. The music started, causing my stomach to flip and sending my heart racing in my chest. The girls lined up, each dropping a kiss on my cheek, before they stepped out the door. With Lexie's help, I straightened my dress and stayed to the side of the door as she moved out onto the deck. Just as the music stopped and the "Wedding March" started, I was joined by a familiar male figure.

"Are you ready, my girl?"

"Let's do this, Daddy."

COOPER

THE SIGHT OF MY LOVE walking down the aisle toward me was the most beautiful thing I had ever seen. My eyes filled, and I didn't bother trying to fight it. Considering we had almost lost him the prior year, it was amazing to see Dale guiding Avery along the path. It was better than any concert or award show, in my mind.

"Fuck, man," I heard Evan mumble beside me.

I nodded to let him know I'd heard him, but I couldn't take my eyes from Avery. This woman had been my everything, and my nothing, for so long. It was hard to believe that, after all this time, she would officially be mine. I was one lucky bastard and I knew it.

Her baby blues leaked down her cheeks, but that didn't take away from her glowing face. The dress she wore clung to her curves and the dip between her cleavage teased and threatened to distract me. I started to feel an erection stir and I had to remind myself we were in front of a shit-ton of people. I had to share her, for now.

When Avery and Dale stopped in front of me, I had to clasp my hands together to keep from reaching out for her. Her father released her arm and whispered a few things in her ear that made her to smile. He then pulled me in for a hug. I returned it fiercely and more tears wet my cheeks. This was the one thing I had wanted more than anything for her; to have her father walk her down the aisle on her wedding day.

"I am so glad I can now officially call you my son," he rasped emotionally. "I couldn't have asked for better for my little girl."

I choked up. There were no words. I wasn't good enough for her, yet I would bust my ass every day for the rest of my life to show them both I was at least minutely worthy. I squeezed him one more time before he stepped back. He placed Avery's hand in mine and moved to sit down in the front row. My bride gripped my hand affectionately and I threw her a reassuring smile before we turned to Maggie.

We had opted for a justice of the peace in our backyard, with our close friends and family, rather than a large church wedding with a reception at some fancy venue. It was more intimate and exactly what she wanted. The security had been a bear, but we made it work by putting up temporary fencing. Avery had been left in the dark about the few glitches, and now that I could see how nervous she was, I was glad she hadn't had more to worry about.

"We are here today to join this woman and this man in matrimony," Maggie started.

I don't remember much about the ceremony. I was too caught up in how gorgeous Avery looked, and about the fact that my childhood dreams were now coming true. The woman beside me would be my wife; she would carry my last name. I'm not sure I would ever get used to that idea. I said the words I was told to repeat, and listened while she said hers. The part I had been waiting for finally came.

"You may kiss the bride," Maggie said.

I could do this part. I flashed Avery a wolfish grin and lowered her into a dip before sealing my lips over hers. I wasn't about to be distracted by the crowd; if anything, the catcalls had me deepening the kiss. I tilted my head and when my wife's lips parted on a sigh, I dove my tongue in to stroke against hers. The passion had her melting against me and her nails biting into my shoulders through my dress shirt. Before I could get lost in the kiss any further, I slowed it down and pulled back, resting my forehead against hers.

"That was cruel, Cooper Hall," she whispered, her eyes opening.

"Just a little tease for later," I whispered back.

Standing us back up, we turned to the crowd, everyone erupted into applause, as Maggie was finally able to officially pronounce us husband and wife. I laughed, as Avery's face turned three shades of red. Grabbing her hand, I threaded our fingers together and led her back between the rows of chairs, to the house. The wedding party would regroup there so we could go out back and do pictures, and the guests would enjoy a cock-tail hour as they waited.

The pictures seemed to take forever, but I think it was mostly because I wanted to pull off the tie I was wearing. Avery had wanted certain ones done, so I just went with the flow. I groaned and rolled my eyes when I saw Evan take a sip from the flask I had given him as a groomsman gift. I wanted a drink, but where I hadn't had anything in just over a year, I was hesitant. He wiggled his eyebrows at me and offered it.

My eyes wandered to where Avery was posing for photos with the girls. Hers met mine and she smiled. Julie handed her a shooter of some sort, and she looked down at it then back at me.

We hadn't said we wouldn't drink, so I nodded at her. Taking the container from Evan, I took a quick swig, closing my eyes as the liquid burned on the way down. It tasted good, yet I didn't feel the need for more. I handed it back.

"You don't miss it?" Chris asked, stepping up on my other side.

"What's that?" I asked with a chuckle, as Lexie, Julie, Jen, and Abby picked up Avery and her hundred-pound dress for a picture.

"The alcohol." He gestured to the flask now resting in Evan's back pocket.

"Nope," I replied. "I mean, yeah, I get the desire for it once in a while, but it's not an aching need type of deal anymore. I can live without it."

He nodded, happy with the answer I gave him. I was over the drinking and partying part of my life. I didn't need it to be a good musician or to put on a good show. Now, looking down at the black titanium band on my fourth finger, I had everything I wanted. My career, my friends, my family, Avery as my wife. I could battle anything with what I had. I didn't need the alcohol to escape: I didn't need to escape anything anymore.

We finished up and went back to the house. The remainder of the day flew by as we ate, danced, and socialized. It was chaotic, crazy, and perfect. If anything was amiss, we didn't know it and I didn't want to. I was high on my wife's smile, laughter, and the way her body moved with her wedding gown. It was getting harder and harder to hide my arousal when she would push up against me during a song, then sashay away.

"I think it's time to get you out of that damn dress," I growled in her ear as she backed her butt into my erection during a pop song.

"There are still a lot of people here," she started to argue, then let out a purr when I wrapped my arms around her to hold her flush against my body, and push against her with my hips.

"The house is empty," I reminded her, trailing a path of nibbles down her bare neck when I moved her hair.

"Let's go," she hissed. "*Now.*"

That was all I needed. I took her hand in mine and tugged her through the crowd, not even stopping to say goodbye to anyone along the way. Nodding to Evan, I opened the flap of the heated tent and let her go out ahead of me. The chill in the air instantly caused goose bumps on her arms. I pulled her into my arms for a quick kiss to warm her up, and was rewarded with a bite on my lip and her hand caressing the front of my pants.

"Okay, let's go," I urged, taking her hand in mine again.

Mikey opened the door for us when we got to the back of the house. No words, just a nod, letting us know everything was good. I shook his hand on the way by, and followed Avery to the bedroom, neither of us stopping until we were in the room and the door was closed behind us.

The room was bathed in soft light and rose petals were scattered everywhere. A soft smell wafted up from the flowers, and the combination of that and Avery's cherry perfume was intoxicating. She planted her feet when she saw everything, and I took the opportunity to pull her hair together and place it over her shoulder so it cascaded down her chest. My fingers danced across her bare shoulders, around to her shoulder blades, and finally to the zipper at the back of the dress. Her sigh urged me to keep going.

I slowly drew the zipper down, trailing open-mouthed kisses down her back as the fabric revealed her skin to me. Her hands came around and gripped my pant legs. I rubbed my erection against her butt gently, eliciting a moan from deep within her. When I reached the end of the zipper, she was clad only in a tiny whisper of lace. I pulled the dress down enough for her to step out of it, and picked it up to lay it gently across a chair in the corner. Turning back around, I found her lying on the bed, watching me lustfully. Her boots, panties, and jewelry were all that remained.

I undressed, moving slower than I wanted, just to torment her. She wiggled and moaned. Moving to the bed, I ran my hands up her legs and then pulled her boots off, one at a time, lingering at the tender skin on her inner thighs. The strip of underwear she wore left little to the imagination, she was wet and ready. Unable to hold it any longer, I pulled off the garment and climbed between her legs.

My hands found hers and anchored us to the bed as she wrapped her legs around me. I moved to her opening, so happy I was bare and could feel her against me. Avery and I had decided that starting a family was in the cards sooner rather than later. No more protection and no more birth control. On top of that, she made me go the entire last month without sex, something about it being romantic. I was a fucking ticking time bomb, but I was determined to keep things slow as I entered her.

"Please, Coop," she pleaded, as I languidly slid in and out of her warm folds, never fully penetrating.

I chuckled, barely holding back the load that was threatening to erupt from my body. I wanted this moment to last forever. Avery's gorgeous wavy long hair was fanned out across the pillows as she tossed her head back and forth. Her eyes were glazed over in passion, and her mouth was slightly open in a moan. Sweat glistened on the curves of her body.

She was mesmerizing.

I stilled my movements once I was sheathed to the hilt, locked inside her, relishing what a fucking lucky son of a bitch I was. That morning, when she came down the aisle toward me in a flowing white dress and a loving smile, I thought she was truly the most beautiful I had ever seen her. This was definitely a close second. My wife, naked except for her diamonds – my diamonds, my promise – wrapped around her finger, and me, bare, wrapped up in her heat, as we started our life together and our own family. Life didn't get any better than this.

Acknowledgments

FIRST AND FOREMOST, I NEED TO thank the person that never lets me give up. The man that pushes me to keep going even when I want to sit in the corner and cry like a baby. Justin, you are my everything and I couldn't have chased this dream without you by my side. I love you more than you will ever know.

My book team, Shauna Kruse, BT Urruela, MGBook-Covers & Design, and T.E. Black Designs, you are the best! I was so blessed to have connected with each and every one of you for this book. I can't tell you how much I appreciate your patience with me while I figure out all the moving parts to this industry. You've all been a wealth of knowledge and I'm looking forward to working with you all again in the future!

Jenn Wood, my editor, my savior. I couldn't have picked a better person to work with me on my book babies and I don't know what I would do without you. You've wiped my tears and loved the characters as much as I have. You've let me, be me. That means more to me than you realize.

Alex Grayson and Heather Lyn, my fellow author ladies, you were the first two to take me under your wings and to answer my never-ending questions. The messages you have both sent mean more to me than I can put into words. You've kept me going on some days and for that I thank you.

Jen Harris and Jessica Woodcock, my cheerleaders from the beginning. There are no sentences, phrases, or words for the love that I hold for you two. You've always made me push my boundaries and never given up on me. Hope you are ready to continue this journey because I'm just getting started.

Katreana Youland, my person, the one that lets me talk about my characters as though they exist in the real world. You have been such a great sounding board as I have changed things up. Thank you so much! I love you!

Starr Ochoa, the newest member of my group, my VA, my voice when I don't have one. Thank you, lady, for jumping in as quickly as you have to help me and to share my stories. I look forward to working more with you and watching you chase your dreams. You've got this girl!

My readers, local and worldwide, my reason for writing in the first place. I had only hoped and dreamed that I would be a published author someday, but you've all helped to make that a reality. Your love for my characters has me pushing through the bad days and celebrating the good, your requests for certain stories has me reworking series to get them in, and your excitement over my writing has me living my dream. I love you all and thank you from the bottom of my heart.

About The Author

Marcie Shumway has been writing short stories for others to enjoy since she was in middle school. *The Return* is the fifth book she has published. She is an avid reader herself, who thrives on the many books of her favorite authors.

Marcie resides in a small town in Maine with her loving husband. The two share their home with their cat, Kyzer, and their dog, Dani. They also have two horses, Chance and Dee.